MW01123886

SHERGAR

the IRA Back Story

To Dan,
Enjoy the read

A NOVEL

yours

stead

authorhalstead@AOL.com

Stephen Halstead

Praise for Stephen Halstead's

debut novel

EVERYWHERE SPIRIT

"The world of high-stakes horse racing as told through one jockey's coming of age. The Native American aspect enriches Jock's story, making for an expansive, fulfilling novel. A fascinating story filtered through one man's journey to overcome his past." —*Kirkus Reviews*

"Entertaining, engaging and inspiring, *Everywhere Spirit* will take a tight grip on the bit in your mouth and keep you focused until the very end. Excellent read!"—B.Howard- *Reader's Favorite* (Five Stars)

"Stephen Halstead delivers a wonderful, yet powerful novel in *Everywhere Spirit.* I found this novel fascinating and the insight into the life of an Apache left me in awe."—Lisa Jones- *Reader's Favorite* (Five Stars)

"*Everywhere Spirit* has many attractions for the reader."— Barbara DuBois, author and Poet Laureate of New Mexico, review writer for *El Defensor Chieftain,* Socorro, N.M.

SHERGAR *the* IRA Back Story

by Stephen Halstead

Copyright © 2015 Stephen Halstead. All rights reserved.

Published by: Crystal Dreams Press

No part of this book may be reproduced in any form either written, electronic, recording, or photocopying without written permission of the publisher or author, except in the case of brief quotations embodied in critical articles and reviews, and pages where permission is specifically granted.

This is a work of fiction. All of the characters and events portrayed in this novel are either fictitious or are used fictitiously. Although every precaution has been taken to verify the historical accuracy of the information contained herein, the author and publisher assume no responsibility for any errors or omissions. No liability is assumed for damages that may result from the use of information contained within.

On the cover: General Post Office, Dublin, Ireland

Cover Design by: Laura LaRoche

Interior Book Design: Carolyn Prior, Toronto, ON, Canada

Author: Stephen B. Halstead b.1944-

Trade Paperback   ISBN: 9781591461739

1. Historical—Fiction 2. Horse Racing—Fiction
3. Sports—Fiction 4. Unsolved Mysteries 5. Crime

Published in Canada. Printed simultaneously in the United States of America and the United Kingdom.

CIP data available from the publisher.

Toronto, ON, Canada

Contents

ACKNOWLEDGEMENTS

A never ending thank you goes to Mary Eileen Mostoller for her loving support and undeniable patience. The author is especially grateful to George Brent for befriending him many years ago at Santa Anita, and for inspiring him to write this story. *Go raibh maith agat* Carolyn Prior of Crystal Dreams Press for the opportunity to bring this book to you, the reader.

DEDICATION

To the memory of my mother and father:
Eileen G. Halstead WAAF
Geoffrey B. Murtough RAAF DFC
And for:
Mary Eileen, one of the Sullivan girls.

PREFACE

The Irish War of Independence, much like the American Revolution, was a culmination of oppressive laws, injustice, the denial of fundamental rights and a lack of freedom. Resentment festered for centuries, before the country was galvanized to act in response to the1916 Easter Rising, Padráig Pearse's 'blood sacrifice.' The Irish lacked resources and manpower. Irish America supplied arms. Led by Michael Collins, the Irish Republican Army supplied men. Great Britain had just concluded defending the Crown against the Kaiser. They had a well-trained, disciplined Army tired of war, and an arsenal depleted. The playing field was beginning to level out. The time was right. Someone said, "if you want to start a war, you've got to kill someone." And kill they did.

A half-century later, a teenage exercise rider begins galloping thoroughbreds for a retired, once-famous, matinee idol turned horse trainer. Together they team up, developing a good filly to win a race at first asking, accomplishing a betting coup in the process. A closeness develops, allowing the actor to reveal he left Ireland a wanted man for his service in the IRA. Taking the youth under his wing, the actor regales him with stories about Pádraig Pearse, Collins, the War, right up through The Troubles, until the Dullahan, Ireland's Herald of Death, calls out the movie star's name.

Meanwhile, the rider falls in love with a mixed race woman, whose opportunities in life are restricted by laws limiting basic freedoms to African-Americans. Imprisoned for the murder of her sexually abusing father, she seeks comfort with her celly. Assisted by a sympathetic parole officer and the Black Panthers, she obtains an expungement and a college degree, which paves the way to a job as a social worker, in the UK.

While there, the couple takes advantage of a chance to witness greatness, the victories of Shergar. The rider sees him daily, while employed on the gallops of Newmarket, allowing the reader to become intimately acquainted with Shergar until his kidnapping, purportedly by the IRA.

I met murder on the way -

He had a mask like Castlereagh -

Very smooth he looked, yet grim;

Seven blood-hounds followed him:

All were fat; and well they might

Be in admirable plight,

For one by one, and two by two,

He tossed the human hearts to chew

Which from his wide cloak he drew.

The Masque of Anarchy
by Percy Bysshe Shelley

INTRODUCTION

A sand in your teeth dust bowl caused the driver and passenger to roll up the windows of the oil spewing Corvair. "Well, here it is, Kid. Ellsworth Ranch."

"Ellsworth what?" the teenager asked his father, as he turned the car off the frontage road, up the drive, to the main house.

"An 80 acre ranch with a ¾ mile racetrack surrounding numerous broodmare paddocks. 50 city blocks of thoroughbreds, bred, raised and trained by Rex Ellsworth. Man has an ad in the paper for boys who want to become jockeys. In exchange for room and board, you work on the ranch and he teaches you to ride."

"Dad, I want an education. You said I was going to a new school. I don't want to be a jockey. I don't know anything about horses," said the troubled youngster.

"You soon will. Besides, you hear your mother an' me fighting over money all the time. I'm about to get laid off, and there's four more of you at home. Right now, I couldn't afford to send you to reform school."

A ranch hand meeting their car opened the passenger door. Begging his father not to leave him, his Dad responded. "You'll be taken care of here and learn a skill. Here's your bag of clothes. Now git," he commanded, with all the heartfelt warmth of someone chasing away a stray dog.

"Come now," the ranch hand beckoned, watching a cloud of desert grit, mixed with black smoke, rise from the departing vehicle.

Fifteen years later, and a continent away, the once abandoned teenager would find himself admiring a winged horse.

CHAPTER ONE

GEORGE BRENDAN NOLAN

The 1964 Santa Anita racing season was well under way on a February morning, when a teenage exercise boy rushed between barns, trying to make a living. At two dollars a gallop, he needed ten horses each day to make enough to live on. The country was still reeling from the shock of President Kennedy's assassination, and the advent of all out war in Vietnam was looming. Pulling up his last scheduled mount of the morning, he heard a voice call out, "You got time for one more?"

"Mr. Brent, sure I do. I'll be over at your barn soon as I get this one untacked," came the eager reply.

George Brent was one of a number of Hollywood movie stars who enjoyed life on the backstretch, along with the Lone Ranger's Tonto, Jay Silverheels, Bonanza's Lorne Greene, and Gunsmoke's Dennis Weaver. Funnyman Jack Klugman, I Love Lucy's Desi Arnez, and Kojak's Telly Savalas were all racehorse owners and frequent visitors. Easily mistaken for jockeys, the diminutive actors, Mickey Rooney and Audie Murphy, were daily regulars, when not filming at the studio. Murphy was America's most decorated soldier from World War II. He was a legendary one man army. Awarded the Congressional Medal of Honor, he preferred the anonymity and solitude walking through the barn area offered.

Wearing Levi's with a threadbare seat, almost worn through from the saddle, the exercise boy wore a résumé of his experience. His frayed helmet cover, and boots rubbed thin at the calf, gave him the credentials of a seasoned race-tracker. Approaching George's barn, he was greeted by an affable, handsome gentleman, now in his sixties. He had the distinguished look of greying nobility, and the grace of movement that comes with the practiced art of acting.

"Hey, Jock, over here. I got one all tacked up and bridled. Tell me your name," he said, extending his hand. "You can just call me George."

"Crash," the lad replied to his query.

"Crash? You kidding me?"

"Wish I was. First horse I ever got on ran off with me in the barn area. He propped at full throttle and hurled me onto a manure pile. That's when I got anointed Crash. I can handle just about any horse now, but can't shake the nickname. Stuck with it, I guess. Benedict Harris is my real name, but please call me Crash."

"Never heard of anyone named Benedict in this

country. No one wants to name their kid after the infamous traitor, Benedict Arnold."

"You got that right. But, I was born in England, named after a saint. There's no stigma attached to the name there."

"Well, Crash it is then," George agreed, legging the rider up onto the saddle. "Just lope this filly an easy mile."

"The track will close in fifteen minutes," boomed the loudspeaker.

"We've got time," commented Crash.

When the filly returned, George gave Crash a few dollars and asked him to hand her to the hotwalker to be watered off, until she cooled down.

"Come, sit down," he said, politely. "How long have you been galloping?"

"Almost three years. Started at Rex Ellsworth's ranch in Chino. He's hard on a horse, but gets results. As you probably know, he had Preakness winner Candy Spots, along with handicap stars, Olden Times and Prove It. Rex imported Khaled from the UK, after buying him from His Highness the Aga Khan III. Khaled has already sired sixty stakes winners, including Kentucky Derby winner, Swaps. You could breed a jenny to that stud and get a runner. Anyhow, my old man pulled me out of school, dropped me off outside Ellsworth's and said, 'there you go; now make a life for yourself.'"

"That must have been tough," offered George.

"It was, but hey, I survived, and that's the

name of the game, isn't it? I got to liking horses and got good at galloping. Now, I want to be a jockey. Speaking of survival, do you want to finish our conversation over breakfast? Eating before I gallop churns my stomach, so I'm starved."

"Sure, let's go over to the track kitchen. I have a favorite table beneath the oversized painting of the owner's Big horse. Harry Curland has the concession and he always puts on a good feed. Huge helpings at small prices, just what any racetracker looks for. Harry likes to give a little back. After all, he won the Hollywood Gold Cup with Solidarity.

"Say, I'm used to calling riders, 'Jock,' especially if I can't remember their name. There's a rider around here with a lot of talent, Jacques Travers. Comes by, now and then. Goes by the name, Jock. Anyway, don't mind me if I holler 'Jock,' to get your attention."

"No, I won't mind. Go ahead, some trainers call me Professor. They say whenever I'm not working, I've got my nose stuck in a book. History mostly."

"Why history?" George asked.

"Well, I can learn something. Science fiction might be entertaining, but it's too much of a stretch for me. History, on the other hand, is real, and can predict the future. A series of details based on bygone happenings results in a major event. It's kinda like training a racehorse. If you know he'll run a corker whenever you breeze him five days out, you wouldn't wait seven days before a race. You just got to know what to look for. And, history always seems to repeat itself."

Having passed through the cafeteria line displaying a menu of bacon, ham, eggs and grits, for $1.29, George picked up the tab.

"You know, Crash, I envy you. Ever since I was a boy growing up in Ireland, I wanted to be a jockey. I was born in Shannonbridge, a small village of 400 in County Offaly. My dad found work in County Roscommon, causing us to move onto the other side of the river. When my parents died before my twelfth birthday, I was sent to New York to live with an aunt for a few years. When I returned to Ireland, I was six feet tall. No chance of riding races, so I went to the University of Dublin. While I was there, I did some plays at the Abbey Theater."

"You're Irish? I thought you were an English actor. You don't talk with a brogue. And, the name Brent sounds British."

"That's because the studios wanted me to tone down the Irish accent, as much as I could. The brogue in Roscommon isn't that strong anyway, and the few years in America caused me to mellow it out even more. Other kids teased me too much. As to my name, maybe I'll explain that later. For now, let's just say it's a common practice to have a stage name."

"Did you have a girlfriend when you went to the university?"

"I don't know if I'd say that. There were a few I

went 'walking out' with. You call it 'going steady' here. But, unlike nowadays, back then you were lucky if you saw some ankle. Between Irish mores and the fear based teachings of the Catholic Church, there was no such thing as 'getting to first base.' Even if you could, you had to have a prescription before you could buy a condom, a Church imposed attempt to regulate the impulsive immorality of youth. If that Rx was not effective, deflowered daughters were often sent to Magdalene Houses, to avoid bringing further shame on the family, and to punish the unchaste."

"I've never been able to understand Irish history," Crash interjected, neither interested in baseball or Victorian dating. "It has always seemed so confusing to me. Muddled."

"Would you like me to try and unravel it for you?" George offered.

"Yeah, I know my Irish ancestors emigrated to England during the Potato Famine of the mid-1800's, but beyond that I'm unclear. Our name used to be Hannigan, but someone way back started using Harris, trying to blend in and not antagonize our English hosts, so I am told. I sure don't understand why the people are still fighting, Catholics against Protestants, Irish against Irish, and everyone against the English."

"Well, before I begin, I should tell you I may be biased. That's because I fought in the War of Independence for Ireland."

"What?" asked Crash, clearly startled by this revelation.

"That's right. And for the Irish Republican Army at that."

"No, way! What was the worst thing you saw during the war?" Crash asked, curiously.

"Not just in the war, but before it: the sheer poverty that prevailed throughout the country. That, and the look of despair on the faces of grown men and women. Their dead eyes. During the War, itself, I guess finding prisoners of the Black and Tans dumped in the gutter was the worst. Left for dead, some had been beaten and kicked so hard, entrails hung out their ass."

"Oh, God, how did they survive?" asked Crash, a look of horror on his face.

"Most didn't." Reflecting a moment, George replied, "All we could do was take them home if it was nearby, or to a friend's house so they could be as comfortable as possible in their last days. Too many of Ireland's youth, on the cusp of manhood, wound up this way. A doctor gave them morphine to ease their pain, a priest administered Extreme Unction, bringing peace to their soul. Men can be so cruel, sometimes. That level of evil hardened the resolve of the Irish to be free."

"Tell me more," pleaded the inquisitive youth.

"I had to leave Ireland. Wanted by the British for treason. I was an Irish Republican Army operative in a squad commanded by Michael Collins, a major player in the revolution. When I came to America after the War for Independence, I changed my name from Nolan to Brent," proclaimed the actor. "Then I came to Southern California – land of sun and palm trees. The economy was good, work was plentiful – no wonder everyone seemed to be smiling. I thought I had found heaven. So, I went to Mass every Sunday and prayed I wouldn't be arrested. Hell of a way to live, though, I'll tell you. On the run, constantly looking over your shoulder. Wondering if the guy walking toward you knows who you are.

"For awhile, I played in a jazz band. One gig led to another; the last was at Jack and Charlies on Manhattan's 52nd St. The balcony above the entrance was surrounded by iron lawn jockeys, painted in the colors of famous patrons."

Crash couldn't help himself, asking, "Were your colors up there?"

"No, fame hadn't found me yet," George chuckled, "and I wasn't looking for it. I then fell into the leading role in a stage play, *Abie's Irish Rose*. It was a comedy that ran on Broadway for five years. But, by the time production closed, I had become fascinated with talking pictures. Voice was key, and my agent thought I should have a go at the transition to talkies. He also represented Gloria Swanson. When she came to New York, we had a chance meeting backstage after a performance of *Abie's Irish Rose*. At the time, the twice divorced, Queen of Screen was married to a French film director. I was finishing up my first divorce. We went out a few times, but I wasn't in her league; she was already making and spending $20,000 a week. A million dollars a year, the studios paid her.

Heck, she spent $10,000 a year on lingerie alone."

"That's a lot of money for underwear," smiled Crash.

"That's for sure," George agreed. "Her affairs were legendary. I didn't rate a mention; pushed aside for those who could further her career, like Cecil B. De Mille and Joseph Kennedy. De Mille directed her in a couple of comedies, *Don't Change Your Husband* and *Why Change Your Wife?* Several of her movies were bankrolled by Kennedy, and they traveled the globe together.

"Gloria introduced me to him as a fellow Irish American, not knowing I served in the IRA and was a fugitive. At the time, Kennedy was financing over-budget movies and refinancing production companies about to go under. He put together some mergers to found RKO, a company that later produced some of my pictures. The guy had the midas touch, and was enamored with the glitter of Hollywood."

Crash just took it all in, fascinated by every aspect of George's life.

"Gloria was Kennedy's trophy mistress, a conquest to show off to his Harvard Alumni pals. Hell, the man had a wife and nine kids. The extent of his philandering was matched only by his devoutness to God, and the Catholic Church. Gloria and I didn't see each other again, for a few years. I had married actress Ruth Chatterton, who insisted on visiting Madame Sylvia, a Norwegian fitness guru who was on Hollywood's A-list. She happened to have booked a suite at The New Yorker to provide massages and dietary counseling to her Eastern clientele, Kennedy and Gloria among them. They were leaving the lobby, when our chauffeur pulled up to the portico."

"How was that scene?" asked Crash.

"A little awkward, but nothing I couldn't handle," replied the actor, with an air of self-confidence.

"I didn't realize it at the time, and maybe Gloria didn't either, but she was about to give Kennedy a well deserved boot. Bloody well deserved, I might add."

"You're not saying that because you were jealous, are you?" chided Crash, with a smirk.

"Let me tell you something about that woman. At the time, she was on husband number four, with two more weddings in her future. She ate guys like me for breakfast. Kennedy had financed one of Hollywood's biggest losers, *Queen Kelly*, starring Gloria, of course. It turns out, some of the costs were charged to Gloria's own personal account, which he managed. Also, Kennedy lavished expensive jewelry on her, charging them off to *Queen Kelly*, ultimately sticking Gloria with the bill. It took a few years and an independent audit, but when Gloria found out, she was livid. She didn't care about the money as much as being duped. Kennedy never invested his own money in anything. He was tighter than one of Gene Krupa's drums.

"About the time *Queen Kelly* was released,

I had a chance to changeover from the stage to the cinema, getting the lead in *Under Suspicion*. Here I was, wanted by MI5, starring in a movie with that for a title. Ironic, huh?" George interjected, using American speak.

"Twenty years later, Gloria and I teamed up for a couple of television episodes of Crown Theater, which she hosted. The two of us were in our fifties. I played the lead, co-starring with Gloria. I did a few TV programs after that, but the show with Gloria really marked the end of my career. Another bit of irony; that last show with her was called *A Fond Farewell*.

"I had tamed my accent to where it helped open a few studio doors. Luckily, I had a some good auditions, even though I never had any formal acting lessons. A life of hiding since being a guerrilla in the IRA, and changing my identity, helped train me. After all, doing a good job of acting was a matter of survival."

"You mean you went into hiding in plain sight on a movie screen? Your films were shown in England, no doubt. Wow, that was ballsy!" Crash joked.

"About right," commented George, "But, by that time British intelligence had more than me to worry about. They were forever trying to ferret out the next plot to topple their grip on the Irish people. Are you really interested in all this?"

"Yes, I want to hear about it. You were there. That would be like reading about World War II, when I can ask someone who was in it."

"Well," began George, "in order to really

understand Ireland, you have to go back into her history; learn about significant events and their effect on social change and economics. Learn about her leaders, their vision for change, what they said and did. One such leader was O'Donovan Rossa, an Irish Fenian. I grew up hearing his name often at the dinner table. Soon after the Potato Famine, he founded the Phoenix National and Literary Society, an unlikely name for an organization which had the goal of liberating Ireland by armed force. Two years later, the Society merged with the Irish Republican Brotherhood, known as Fenians. Because of his IRB activities, he was eventually charged with high treason. Sentenced to life at hard labor, he served time in several of Britain's harshest prisons.

"Rossa was released under the Fenian Amnesty Agreement, which called for his exile to America. There, from his home on Staten Island, he continued to be a political influence and began what is known as the 'dynamite campaign,' the organized bombing of British buildings having an economic or political purpose. Britain requested his extradition to stand trial for masterminding the planting of dynamite bombs. America refused. By now, Irish Americans had become a major political force. Rossa died at age 83 after a long illness. Accompanied by a priest, his body was returned to Ireland to be buried.

"Thousands attended his funeral, complete with an armed honor guard of Irish Volunteers. As he lay in state in Dublin City Hall, the green with sunburst, Fenian flag draped across his open casket. Befitting someone held by the people in such esteem, a four-in-hand, horse drawn hearse followed by several carriages, drums and bagpipes, proceeded to Glasnevin Cemetery on the outskirts of Dublin near Finglas. During the ceremony, the magnificent team of horses with erect, black feathered mourning combs atop their heads, stood anxiously, prancing in place, as if waiting for the Dullahan to alight and be on his way.

"A twenty-one gun salute followed the lowering of the casket. Believe you me, the Irish know how to put on a funeral. Rossa's was held on the same day as the Celtic harvest celebration, assuring a large turnout.

"The scholarly Pádraig Pearse, himself a respected revolutionary, delivered a graveside speech, presaging the struggles to come. Here, I keep a copy of it."

Pulling a tattered, worn, folded paper from his wallet, George let Crash read the words he held dear:

The Defenders of this Realm have worked well in secret and in the open. They think they have purchased half of us and intimidated the other half. They think they have foreseen everything, think they have provided against everything; but the fools, the fools, the fools!- they have left us our Fenian dead, and while Ireland holds these graves, Ireland unfree will never be at peace.

—Pádraig Pearse
August 1, 1915

"Let me back up to the Easter Rising in 1916, when I was eighteen, about your age, I'd guess."

"Yes, go on," Crash enthused.

ℤ ℤ ℤ

CHAPTER TWO

EASTER RISING

"The Easter Rising," George continued, "was the culmination of a series of events, like you mentioned, the past predicting the future. Anti-war protests had been going on, since the outbreak of the Great War in 1914. England had instituted conscription at home, with passage of the British Military Act in 1916. But, it was willing to forego the draft in Ireland as long as there were enough volunteers for military duty, and food supplies to the homeland were not disrupted. Irish lads were against British recruitment, and opposed to fighting for Britain's freedom, when Ireland itself was not yet free. To most Irish, the concept of dying for England remained reprehensible.

On Saturday, April 22, 1916, the British Navy intercepted a German merchant ship flying the flag of a friendly nation, instead of the German black, white, and red tricolor. With a cargo of guns and ammunition, its captain scuttled the vessel off Ireland's coast, in the Celtic Sea. Later that same day, a retired British diplomat was captured from a German submarine in Tralee Bay, on the Atlantic Coast of Ireland.

War makes for some strange bedfellows. A proponent of a free Ireland, Sir Richard Casement had been recruiting Irish prisoners of war captured by the Germans in France, with the purpose of forming an invading force against the British. Despite having been knighted by King George for exposing the depredations committed against the people of the Belgian Congo, he was arrested for sedition, returned to Britain and hanged.

It was Casement who brought an end to the horrors endured by the Congolese, whose children were unable to scoop coal from the mines fast enough to satisfy their bosses. To inspire increased productivity in others, fathers were forced to sever their children's hands with a machete. Many bled to death as a result of this diabolical cruelty. In a culture where hunting and gathering were a means of livelihood, the surviving children were destined for a life of suffering.

British intelligence provided the Army names of those involved with the German delivery of weapons. Arrests were imminent. The Irish rebels were not without their spies. Aware death awaited them, the leaders of the Irish Republican forces were compelled to act. In the months beforehand, Pearse, a prolific writer of poems, and several politically like minded friends of poetry, planned an uprising. They referred to it as the Conspiracy of Poets. Appointed Commandant General of the Army of the Irish Republic, Pádraig Pearse led 1500 armed men into Dublin on Easter Monday. Many of the townspeople were away celebrating the holidays, some attending the local horse races at Fairyhouse Racecourse. Pearse's troops were supported by cooks and nurses from a Republican woman's organization. *Fianna Éireann*, a boy scout group, supplied messengers. It was a rag tag army wearing a mix of uniforms from the Irish Volunteers, Irish Citizens Army, and the militia of the Irish Transport and General Workers Union. In place of a uniform, some wore Sam Browne gun belts over their civilian clothes.

Weapons were a museum collection of arms, including pikes and spears, rifles of varying caliber, shotguns, handguns and an assortment of homemade bombs, all designed to maximize bloodshed. Support from a German ground force never materialized. The mere association with Britain's sworn enemy invited retribution, virtually precluding any type of reconciliation. For all intents and purposes, the Irish were considered hooligans, unworthy of respect or compassion. It had always been that way.

The attack on Dublin was defended by a mere 400 British soldiers on duty that Monday. The remainder of the garrison were on leave for the Easter holiday.

Having initially gained control of the General Post Office (GPO), Pearse stood on the steps and read The Proclamation of the Irish Republic, not unlike the American Declaration of Independence. The document contained an acknowledgement of contributions made by Irish Americans for Ireland's cause, stating gratitude for 'the support by her exiled children in America.' A skilled orator, his paced delivery style captivated audiences, unaware the wordsmith they were listening to measured each syllable to compensate for a life-long stutter.

The document went on to proclaim the Irish Republic a sovereign and independent state, declaring a provisional government to administer civil and military matters within the Republic, in trust for the people, until a national government was convened. Soon thereafter, the remaining British garrison of 2,000 soldiers returned. They were joined by another 1,000 re-enforcements arriving by boat on Wednesday. Fierce fighting continued day after day.

Knowing victory would be short lived, Pádraig Pearse and the other leaders hoped that by making a 'blood sacrifice' they would awaken a sense of nationalistic pride in the people. Over 450 were killed and some 2500 wounded. Many were civilians. Surrender came after six days, when the British burned out the GPO. All seven signatories to the proclamation, including Pearse, were imprisoned at Kilmainham, in addition to eight others, deemed co-conspirators. The following day they were court-martialed in proceedings having all the elements of a kangaroo court. The accused could not call witnesses in their defense, could not question the Crown's witnesses, and were denied counsel. Pearse, a barrister, was not surprised. This was the very same type of oppressive conduct, which led to the Rising in the first place."

"Whew, it doesn't get much more kangaroo than that," opined Crash. "Why even bother with a trial?" he asked.

"America." George answered. "Too many Irish here with money and influence. Britain was trying to get the U.S. to join forces with her to defeat the Kaiser."

"So what happened to the prisoners?" Crash wanted to know.

"They were ordered to be executed before a firing squad," replied George. "Within two days all were shot, including Pearse's younger brother, Willie, who had only a minor role in the uprising. Call it guilt by association. Pádraig never had a chance to say goodbye to Willie, a gifted sculptor. A visit by their mother was also denied. Before being taken out into the yard, Pádraig, a former teacher and founder of St. Enda's School, which emphasized the preservation of the Gaelic language, wrote his last words.

"The bespectacled Pearse, already frail, was weakened further by the attack on the GPO and the sleeplessness it brought on him. Letters to Willie, his sister nicknamed Wow Wow, and to his mother, a final poem, along with instructions on his financial affairs and unpublished manuscripts were found and retrieved by those cleaning his empty death cell. As best he could, he wanted to tie up any loose ends.

"He left behind his penned testimony, which he delivered from the dock the previous day. In part, he wrote:

If you strike us down now, we shall rise again and renew the fight. You cannot conquer Ireland. You cannot extinguish the Irish passion for freedom. If our deed has not been sufficient to win freedom, then our children will win It by a better deed.

"Having received Absolution and Holy Communion, Pearse was led down a long corridor in manacles to the stonebreaker's yard. Standing in front of a wall of sand bags, Pádraig Pearse looked directly at the British firing squad, his scornful, accusatory glare unwavering. Quickly blindfolded, he was prepared to die for Ireland as so many others before him, and as so many more would follow. A white square paper target was pinned over his heart.

"Initially, the uprising was unpopular and its leaders were condemned by the people. A crowd jeered and threw rotten vegetables at the prisoners, as they were being marched through the streets to Richmond Barracks for their court-martial. Neighbors and loved ones had been killed. Daily life had been disrupted, and their city was destroyed. Eventually though, the blood sacrifice made by so many pushed apathy aside, and reawakened a renewed sense of nationalism as predicted by Pearse."

"Hey, man, that's about all I can absorb in one day. I've got a date meeting me at the Arcadia bowling alley tonight. We won't be 'walking out.' Gonna try and get laid," said the impish youth.

"Don't do anything stupid," cautioned George. "See you tomorrow, if you show up."

"Oh, I'll show. I want to hear more."

Always reliable, Crash arrived early the next morning, displaying his stable license for track security, before being allowed inside the barn area.

"Hi, Crash," George greeted, as his exercise rider ambled down the shedrow. "Get on that grey filly you galloped yesterday. Let her quicken down the stretch."

Upon her return, George remarked the filly went great. "Every day is like another step forward. My hotwalker seems to have vanished. After I get her cooled out, we can get a bite to eat, from the tack room fridge, then it's story time."

"Okay by me. I'm all ears."

Sitting on a bale of bleached, yellow, premium straw, Crash listened as George picked up from where he left off the previous day. "I'm no historian, so I'm only going to repeat what I learned in school. One thing about the Jesuits, though, they school you good," he said, breaking into the vernacular of the racetrack.

"Anyhow, you've got to go back to the twelfth century, when the first and only English Pope was head of

the Catholic Church. Pope Adrian IV bestowed the
mantle, Lordship of Ireland, upon King Henry II,
essentially passing title of all Ireland's Celtic land to
England's King, exempting any Catholic owned property. From that day forward, for the next 700 years,
daily life for the average Irishman and his family was
insufferable. Resentment festered through generations until there was only hate. Over the next four
centuries, the Irish witnessed the dismantling of
their language and culture. They would be required
to adopt English ways and customs, much like the
changes forced upon Native Americans.

"And like America, the country was politically unstable. Its inhabitants were seen as
third world savages, ignorant and undeserving.
Throughout time, the English have always
viewed indigenous peoples of other lands with
contempt, as sub-human. And, worse, they
considered whatever the native's possessed to
be theirs for the taking, a self serving inter-
pretation of the *Doctrine of Manifest Destiny*.
The British were ahead of the times, applying
America's nineteenth century policy on expan-
sion, long before the New World was discovered.

"Incredibly, in the 1600's, a Puritan named
Oliver Cromwell came to power, and things got
worse. His first order of business, after being
designated Lord Protector of England, was to
sign a warrant for the execution of King Charles I.
Next, Cromwell ordered the massacre of Irish
Catholics. By confiscation or proclamation, he
redistributed six thousand Catholic estates to

those English who had supported his rise to power."

"I read a little about him in high school; not even a chapter though. More like a paragraph. From what I remember, he was a real dick," interrupted Crash, expressing an opinion held by many of Cromwell's subjects at the time. "I read he was both praised and vilified, while in office. He was essentially a dictator and hated Catholics, especially Irish ones, as much as Hitler hated Jews. Cromwell's killing spree was nothing short of genocide."

"Well, young man, you do seem to know your history. That whole Catholic hate thing has carried over to the present day, with the Northern Ireland Protestants under British rule. Unlike Germany's Jews, Catholics didn't wear a Star of David to be identified. But, out of habit, they would cross themselves, and be marked as clearly as if they wore a yellow star. To leave mass on Ash Wednesday and forget to wipe the ashen cross off their forehead was oftentimes a fatal error.

"When you have hate passed on from generation to generation, reconciliation is almost impossible. Look at the Jews and Arabs. I bet most couldn't give you a good reason for their hate. It's generational. People in this country hate because of someone's skin color, or if they are homosexual. That may change in our life time, a little anyhow, but not completely.

"Cromwell died from a urinary tract infection

five years after coming to power. He was buried at Westminster Abbey along with deceased royals. When the monarchy was restored to power, they ordered Cromwell's body exhumed, then publicly hanged posthumously. The corpse was beheaded, then reburied separately in a Sussex graveyard, with the head displayed on a pike outside the castle gate, thus foiling his body's restoration on the Day of Resurrection."

Returning to the topic, George continued, "did you ever wonder where the hostility between the Irish Catholics and the Protestants came from?"

"You mean other than what you've just told me. My dad said it always was, and always will be. He said it was just like the Jews and Arabs, Shiites and Sunnis, or the Hutu and Tutsi in Africa. They are all savages. That's how he put it. And he said there is nothing to be done."

"I disagree. But, each side has to first understand the other's history and the role they themselves played in it, before any meaningful peace process can begin."

"So can you tell me in twenty-five words or less about their histories?" Crash questioned.

"I don't know jack about Africa or the Middle East. But, I do know something about Ireland. I was willing to give my life for her, although at the time, I really didn't understand why. I knew most of us hated the Protestant British, and we wanted to be ruled by ourselves. I think that's every man's dream. As a matter of fact, the dominant Irish political party, *Sinn*

Féin, translates to 'we ourselves.' Look at the American Revolution. England learned nothing from that experience.

"So the short answer to your question is the Irish Catholics, their language and political role eliminated, were now forced to talk English, while working their former lands for English landlords, paying rent and taxes on the pittance they earned."

"I didn't count, but you might have gone over twenty-five," smiled Crash. "At any rate that must have caused some serious resentment."

"Yes, and it grew exponentially from one generation to the next, spurred on by starvation and disease, festering until coming to a head at the time of the Easter Rising," George added. "Resentment flourished into downright hate, the predominant emotion during Ireland's struggle to be free. I want to show you something. I'll bring it with me tomorrow."

The next day George showed Crash an old scrapbook, marked "Ireland."

"I've got a bunch more for Hollywood, full of newspaper clippings, *Variety* articles, and reviews. The small one for the racetrack I keep here in the tack room. I'll never win enough races to get the win photos and press clippings to fill it. But, hey so what?" he asked rhetorically, not expecting a reply, stating, "I enjoy what I'm doing."

"Look at this," directed George, as he produced a yellowed newspaper story about O'Donovan

Rossa's funeral. This was the first big event I went to after I returned to Ireland from America. Read it from here down," he said, pointing mid-page.

The oratory skills of Pádraig Pearse were recorded next to a penciled sketch of Rossa's casket and graveyard monuments. Next to an obelisk was *The Grieving Angel* drawn in detail, a flower engraved above the inscription, its blossom broken at the stem. Sketched beneath a large yew tree, Pearse stood speaking:

> *We pledge to Ireland our love, and we pledge to English rule in Ireland our hate. This is a place of peace, sacred to the dead, where men should speak with all charity and with all restraint, but I hold it a Christian thing, as O'Donovan Rossa held it, to hate evil, to hate untruth, to hate oppression; and hating them, to strive to overthrow them.*

George was a pacifist at heart, frequently saying he wished the Republicans and members of Parliament could have agreed to a date certain for all Ireland to be free. If he had his druthers, he liked to say, using slang he'd picked up when on location in Australia, "I'd have sat those pommies down and reminded them, throughout history, oppressed people have always risen up to rebel against those who rule them. Sooner or later they succeed. So why not just turn Ireland back to her sons and daughters now, and save the grief on both sides?"

"Grief," the teenager repeated. "How about bloodshed? Couldn't you or some peace negotiator have presented that option to the British?" asked Crash, somewhat naïve to the ways of men in power.

"Never work," said George. "They had us in a vise for over seven hundred years. If they couldn't keep Ireland, they would just as soon crush her. Just like bullies everywhere, except they are thugs in morning coats and top hats.

"Britain's Parliament didn't have to take a poll of the Irish people to assess their mood, or wonder if hostilities were coming to a boil. They needed only listen to the speeches of Pádraig Pearse, heeding his foreboding words, to avoid violence. Alas, it was not within them," George lamented with solemnity, genuinely saddened, as he recalled the time.

CHAPTER THREE

HOLLYWOOD PARK

Racing at Santa Anita was coming to a close, with the Spring/ Summer meeting at Hollywood Park set to begin.

"George, are you going to train today?" asked Crash.

"No, I'm shipping across town. The van will be here at eleven. Plan to be bedded down in a new barn this afternoon. Find me tomorrow, I'm in 12A."

Track management concedes to the superstitious trainers by omitting references to the number 13 on barns and stall doors, reasoning that in a game where luck is paramount, why take unnecessary chances.

"I'll be there," Crash assured him.

One hour away, in the City of Inglewood, was beautiful Hollywood Park, promoted as the track of Lakes and Flowers. Every year they held a beauty contest, where the winners of Los Angeles suburban beauty pageants vied for the title of Goose Girl. Last year's winner, Miss El Monte, crowned Miss Santa Monica. Themed in a Dutch Goose Girl costume, a white triangular bonnet took the place of a tiara.

The next morning Crash breezed the grey filly for George, a tick under a minute for 5/8 ths.

"How did she gallop out past the wire?" asked George.

"Good. Real strong," came the reply.

George subscribed to the belief of many good trainers, that a strong gallop-out was indicative of fitness, ready for a top effort; the actual time of the drill less important. Eager to cash a bet, his exercise boy asked when she was going to race.

"In about two weeks. One more breeze will set her on tilt. She'll be crying to run."

"Let me know, I'll try not to pester you. Who are you going to ride? Has she ever run before?"

"Goddammit, Kid, you already are pestering me. You're worse than some jock agent," snapped George.

"Sorry, I didn't mean to annoy you," apologized Crash.

"Don't worry, I'll give you a heads up," promised George, sounding less aggravated.

Over the last few months, the two had grown close. George was happy to have a steady exercise boy with talent, who showed up every day. Crash couldn't get enough history from a man who had actually lived it.

Days were often filled with stories of the IRA and Britain's oppression of the Irish people.

Occasionally, conversation would foray into the world of Hollywood on those rare times Crash asked George about his film career, some sixty plus movies. Since retiring in 1952, he enjoyed a sense of anonymity, content to be a horse trainer.

CHAPTER FOUR

FEM-AHLI

The underage Crash used a fake ID to get into the Gold Cup lounge on Century Boulevard, a few blocks from the stable gate. There he met an attractive young woman of mixed race, a few years older than himself. Her dark hair, coarse at the roots, combed into a shapely bob at her neckline, accentuated her Caucasian features. She introduced herself as Fem-Ahli.

"Never heard that name before," Crash said, inquisitively, as they took their drinks to a gold tufted Naugahyde booth.

"Yes, it's a little strange. I pronounce it the way my mother and grandmother do. Here, I'll write it down on a cocktail napkin for you," she said, beginning to print F-E-M-A-L-E.

"That's female!" exclaimed Crash. "It's obvious you are one," he stated, in a roundabout compliment.

"Well, you have to know my mother was only fifteen when I was born. Dropped out of school in the seventh grade and got pregnant at fourteen by my uncle."

"What? Her own brother?" Crash asked, shocked.

"Yeah, that's right. Sick, huh?" Fem-Ahli said, not expecting an answer. "I grew up in the ghetto, Watts, not far from here, on the other side of Inglewood. My grandmother says, when my mom came home from the hospital, she said the nurses named me Fem-Ahli. When I started junior high, I saw it written on my birth certificate. I asked her why that name. True story; she said the hospital gave me the name and put it on the plastic bracelet they sent me home with."

"Oh, my God!" exclaimed Crash, amazed anyone could be so naïve.

"It's been a source of embarrassment at times, especially on job applications. But, it pales when compared to being the daughter of incest."

Crash didn't know what to make of all this. Fem-Ahli was certainly pretty, intelligent, and not the least bit shy. Crash doubted he, nor anyone else he knew, would reveal such intimate details unless tortured." He was smitten.

"Do you have a nickname?" Crash asked, hoping.

"Yeah, my friends call me Grace."

"Good, just count me as a friend, Grace," he said, relieved he wouldn't have to ask for Fem-Ahli, whenever he called, as she passed him her number.

"Do you work around here, in Inglewood?"

"I clean houses for a living. A lot of jobs aren't available to me. Colored businesses don't want to hire me because I'm too White, and Whites have told me I look too Negro. My nose is a little flat, and my brown eyes give me away. Shop owners say customers will stop coming to their store, once they realize the business has hired a Colored."

Crash was listening attentively, then commented,"That's the most ridiculous thing I've ever heard of. Besides, your nose is cute. How about mine?" he asked, pointing to his aquiline profile.

"Well it looks like it could belong to Geronimo," she giggled, "but I don't think God made any blue-eyed, fair skinned Indians."

"Only in Oklahoma," Crash added, laughing, in a reference to all the White people of that state, who claimed some minimal Native American heritage to obtain benefits. "So do you live here, too?" he asked.

"No chance of that. Inglewood has a 'Sunset' ordinance. No Colored people are allowed before dawn or after sunset. That way we can continue to work as domestics or gardeners, but not live here."

"That's unbelievable!" Crash exclaimed, shaking his head in disgust.

"It's true," Grace reaffirmed.

Looking at the clock above a display bottle of Mezcal, Crash realized twilight had begun. He pondered out loud about the unfortunate worm at the bottom of the bottle before saying, "I have to get up early. I'm staying in a tack room at a trainer's barn. Did you drive here?"

"Walked over from the last house I cleaned."

"Well, I'll drive you home, wherever it is. I've

got an old Buick. It's not much, but it gets me around," he said, apologetically.

"You can't. Way too dangerous for a White boy to drive a Colored girl home into Watts. You'll never get out alive. I hear the rumblings on the street. Young trouble makers are itching to make war. So many will take you down, no one will know who killed you. Remember, you heard it here first. Watts will literally blow the lid off discrimination."

"I'll take your warning to heart. So how will you get home?"

"The bus. I can pick it up here at Crenshaw and Century, and it lets me off near my door," said Grace, describing her route.

"Be safe," Crash cautioned, hugging Grace good-bye.

The next day, a Saturday, he telephoned when training hours were over. They agreed to meet at Bob's Big Boy hamburger diner near the track. Sitting in a booth, they waited for someone to take their order. A half-hour went by. Others came, ate, and left. White others. Crash spoke to the manager, who promised someone would take their orders 'soon.'"

Fifteen minutes passed before Crash questioned a horse trainer sitting nearby, "What's going on?"

"This must be your first time here," he guessed. "They don't serve Coloreds in here. They're afraid, if they do, the place will fill up with them. Mostly at lunch time. By the dinner hour, they have to be out of town. Wouldn't have time to eat before dark. But, White folk still ain't comin' in to eat off dishware Coloreds ate from. It's as much about economics as it is prejudice."

"Well fuck 'em. We'll leave," said Crash, astonished at the audacity and rudeness of some adults. The couple crossed Prairie to a deli and split a foot long sub. Talking some more, Crash learned Grace's mother supports her other four children with welfare and food stamps. Their fathers were unknown. The father/uncle still lived in the two bedroom, stucco, wood framed rental with his sister. This was Grace's home.

"Does your uncle ever come onto you?"

"From time to time," mumbled Grace, staring downward.

"What happens?"

"I give into him. He tells me he'll go to my sister's bed if I don't."

"Have you told your mother?"

"What? They sleep together. I'm sure she knows. She's just glad to get a night off."

"Jesus, that's outrageous. Why don't you call social services or the police?"

"First off, the mostly White LAPD won't come into Watts on a domestic violence call. Too dangerous. Yeah, I know it's child abuse, but they log it in as domestic. They're afraid their presence in the neighborhood will be the spark that ignites the community powder keg. There is so much anger and resentment. Besides that, no one is going to testify against him, including me. Before trial, he'll get bail because the jails are overcrowded. One of his dope selling friends will spring for it. He'll come home and beat the shit out of us. I've been through it and seen it in the neighborhood time and again."

Oh, Man, I wish I could help you. I don't know what I can do," said her frustrated friend.

"For now, just listen. Sometimes, I just need a shoulder to cry on. But, I carry a lot of baggage, and if you have any sense, you should run, not walk the other way."

Crash recalled a time when he burned his fingertips playing with matches. Now he was about to handle a flame thrower. He felt like a moth drawn to fire.

"It's starting to get late. The buses don't run much through Watts after dark. I better catch one now, while I can." Waiting for the LA Transit No. 8, destination Lynwood, the couple arranged to meet at the Gold Cup the following Monday afternoon. Before boarding, Grace kissed her friend good-bye.

Returning to his tack room after picking up dinner to-go at the track kitchen, Crash turned on his black and white portable, shifting the rabbit ears to clear the snow blurring the seven o'clock news. Police in Georgia and Alabama, dressed in riot gear, were trying to disperse peaceful marchers. Truncheons, vicious dogs and fire hoses countered songs of freedom. Some were killed, many were wounded in scenes rivaled only by images from Cape Town, the capital of Apartheid.

Crash had a restless night, unable to stop thoughts of Grace's plight. He realized part of the problem lay in the public's view that "these people" are little more than savages, undeserving of White man's laws. 'Let them rot in the jungle of their making,' was a comment often heard. Crash couldn't help thinking it was an environment White America had created for them.

After galloping a few for George Brent that Sunday morning, the two began to discuss Grace and her family life. George was appalled. "You watch yourself," he warned. "Anytime someone sees you as upsetting how things are, you become a target.

"Your description of last night's television news has many similarities with our cause in Ireland, when I was in the IRA. Discrimination, oppression, laws enforced against some, not others, all serve to instigate riot and revolution. Read about the Czar's overthrow in Russia or Pancho Villa and the Mexican Revolution. When people are marginalized by economic and social disparity, they eventually turn on their persecutors.

"That's what the Freedom Marches are about. Their leaders see a revolution coming unless Civil Rights laws are enacted, and more importantly they are upheld. Watts is so volatile, I don't think they can wait. Perhaps it will be a good thing though. Congress will get a glimpse of what will happen across the nation, if changes aren't achieved."

CHAPTER FIVE

COMPTON

After training hours, Crash decided to find an apartment to rent, at least until the race season ended. He planned to invite Grace to share a place, to allow her to break out from the life she was forced to live. He didn't bother looking in Inglewood, driving instead to the next town over, Hawthorne. There, at the limits he was greeted by a forbidding city sign warning:

Nigger, Don't Let the Sun Set On You In Hawthorne.

Good God, he thought, I'm in Southern California, might as well be in Mississippi. At least someone dared paint over the sign's most offensive term, Crash said to himself.

Although the city removed the sign and repealed the Sunset law by the time the 1968 Civil Rights Act was passed, it remained in effect surreptitiously. Real estate agents and landlords discriminated against people of color, telling them the property was sold or rented, a practice known as *realty steerage*. Employers told non-white job applicants the position was filled. Police harassed drivers of color, manufacturing reasons for pulling them over, deterring them from entering the city. Over the years to come, Civil Rights based litigation would have to take place for meaningful change to occur.

The few who would consider renting to Coloreds, did not approve of unmarried couples living together. Options were limited in the bigot driven culture of 1960's Los Angelenos. Fifteen miles from Inglewood, Crash found a furnished mother-in-law studio. Judging from the construction, no building permit had been issued. This suited Crash, as there was less likely to be an objection when Grace arrived. That night in the Gold Cup, Crash told of his day.

"But, I can't just move in with you," objected Grace. "I have to think of my sister."

"Maybe it will do you good. Your skin is light enough, you can probably get a job in Compton that pays better than housecleaning. You could visit your family after work. Just be sure and tell Uncle to leave your sister alone."

"I'm scared," Grace added.

"Don't worry, I'll sleep on the couch," assured Crash.

"That's not what I meant, silly. What if I really like living with you? What will happen at home?

Where will I go when the racing season ends?"
asked Grace, her head spinning.

"Well, maybe we'll go down to Del Mar. It
starts up at the end of July and runs through
Labor Day. I don't have all the answers. Maybe
everything at home will go alright, but whatever,
you need to get out before your life is ruined."

"Okay, we'll see, but if things go bad at home,
our honeymoon will be over," she replied, smiling;
the tone eerily foreboding.

True to his word, Crash bunked out on the
couch. A short time later, Grace sat down beside
him. Stirring, he looked up. "I can't sleep. Come
into my bed and hold me," she beckoned.

Crash wasn't sure if he was confusing admira-
tion with love; though certain he was very fond
of Grace, as she took his hand, leading the way.

Soon, their eyes were locked in lust, lips
arousing carnal senses. He stormed her heart.
Urgently, her feelings for him became known.
Hands fondled, searching for pleasure. Dark
pigment surrounded each nipple, contrasting
with her smooth caramel skin. Grace took him in
her mouth, eliciting a plea to, "slow down." She
pushed back, guiding him between her thighs.
Illuminated by the street lamp outside, her skin
glowed golden. Finding the heat inside, Crash
could no longer restrain himself, bringing her to
orgasm; the radio playing The Drifters' *Save the
Last Dance for Me*, spun by deejay Art Laboe on
station KRLA. Quietly holding each other, the
pair descended into a deep sleep.

The couple fell into a routine. Crash galloped horses in the morning, hanging out at the races in the afternoon. George often told stories about life in Ireland, occasionally mentioning his time in stardom. Crash sensed George had some regrets about leaving his home, the IRA, Michael Collins and his other comrades, before Independence was attained. George made it clear, he took this chapter in his life very seriously. It was hard for him to give a similar level of importance to his accomplishments in Hollywood.

Each day, Grace walked to the Ralph's Supermarket, where she was a cashier-in-training. Afterward, she would make the round trip bus ride to Watts to check on her family. More than once, she refused her Uncle, warning him the children would be removed if anything happened to her sister, trusting the threat of losing his meal ticket would keep him at bay.

On a stormy morning, electricity in the air, the grey filly was more than a handful, bucking and leaping upon her return to the barn. When Crash dismounted, George announced two suits were at the end of the shedrow, waiting to talk to him.

"Who are they?" Crash asked.

"Don't know, didn't ask. Just assumed they were from the Racing Commission. Did you get into some jackpot, over at Santa Anita?"

"No, Man. I'm good. I'll go see what they want," Crash replied anxiously, striding toward the men, who promptly pulled out their shields, identifying themselves as detectives from LAPD.

"Homicide Unit," said the older one. "This is Sergeant Owen, I'm Lieutenant Enright. Could we step into this room and talk?" he said, motioning toward the tack room. Moving aside some saddles and turning over some empty water buckets, the three were seated.

Making an effort not to be confrontational, Crash proclaimed he hadn't killed anyone.

"We didn't say you did," declared the lieutenant.

"Fine. Then there is no need for me to be here." Crash stood to go.

"Hold on," commanded the sergeant. "We've come to tell you we have your girlfriend in custody for her uncle's murder."

"Not just her uncle. He's her father, too!" advised Crash.

"What?" the sergeant responded. Even this jaded veteran of the streets was unable to conceal his shock. Informing the young rider, it was Grace, herself, who reported the crime, they asked if there was anything they needed to know about about her relationship with her uncle. Crash told them of the long history of incest and the uncle's threats to violate her sister. They gave assurances the information would go into their report and, no doubt, be seen as mitigating circumstances.

"So what comes next?" asked Crash.

"Most likely bail will be set high because it is a capital offense," answered Lieutenant Enright. It's doubtful she will even be able to meet the bail bondsman's ten percent, even if she can come up with the collateral. A public defender will be appointed and hopefully the judge will get to hear the whole story." Even the LAPD was not beyond compassion, Crash thought.

Depressed by all that had transpired, he told George he was going home to pack up, and move back to the track. County jail visits are restricted to an approved short list, reserved for lawyers and family. Months went by before Crash learned a plea bargain had been reached. After entering a guilty plea to voluntary manslaughter, Grace was sentenced to eight years in prison, to be served at CIW, the California Institute for Women at Frontera in Chino. Time off for good behavior would cut the term in half. Regardless, the conviction would forever impact her life.

Crash spent the remainder of Hollywood Park galloping, and listening to Irish history. He never tired of either.

CHAPTER SIX

THE WORKHOUSE

One morning, George began, "If you think life under Cromwell was bad, in time it became unbearable. Over the next two hundred years, Ireland was made a part of the United Kingdom and the Irish Parliament was dissolved. Penal laws prohibited Catholics from holding office, voting, buying land, and the freedom to attend their Church or a faith based school. The laws were based on the presumption Catholics were disloyal to the Crown, lacked religious faith, and were untruthful.

"This latter presumption made prosecution of Catholics just that much easier. On trial for stealing a loaf of bread, a Catholic denying his guilt was presumed to be lying. Likewise any Catholic witnesses, who came forward to testify on his behalf, were automatically deemed to be untruthful, irrespective of any oath, based solely on their religion. It was a big hurdle for the accused to overcome.

"Imprisonment was certain. The purpose of the laws was to strengthen the establishment of the Church of England. With over seventy-five per cent of Ireland baptized Catholic, the laws were a recipe for revolt.

"No Catholic could hold a civil service job, serve on a jury, work in the legal profession or as a constable or sheriff. When the Nazis came to power in the 1930's, Jews were similarly discriminated against, prohibited from performing civil service jobs, jury service, law enforcement or the judiciary.

"A Catholic refusing to work on a Holy Day was subjected to an unmerciful flogging. Other punishments ranged from a fine, forfeiture of property, official deportation to far away islands like Barbados, and death to those who refused to leave, when ordered to self-deport.

"Unemployment sky-rocketed, affecting the majority of the male population, now unable to provide for their families. For those willing to renounce their faith and embrace the Church of England, a pension or separate government maintenance was provided. Poor Laws were enacted in response to the Draconian Penal Laws, which impoverished most of the nation, destroying the economy."

"How crazy was that?" interjected, Crash.

"More than we could ever know," replied George, as he continued to narrate his country's turmoil. "England's solution to such abject poverty was a system of workhouses, built throughout the nation. Completely contained, some housed up to seven thousand people, straining water, cooking and sanitation beyond healthy limits. Most were run like an indoor Nazi concentration camp. Death and disease were rampant. Facing certain starvation or denying their souls eternal salvation by renouncing Catholicism, most chose the workhouse. Once a family entered, it was broken apart. Children and adults were separated by gender, forbidden to leave the building."

"Sounds like Dachau to me," said Crash, agreeing with George's opinion.

"Believe it or not, there was another level of horror," added George. "Fever hospitals were erected to stop the spread of cholera raging throughout Europe. Once contracted, few survived. The Irish were particularly vulnerable. Their immune system weakened by years of hunger, some died of dehydration hours after onset. Others were literally herded into hospitals or buildings dedicated to provide treatment of the disease.

"Virtually everyone performing nursing care was infected. Vendors refused to make deliveries. Caregivers soon took the place of patients. The dying were ministered by the walking dead. Admission to a fever hospital, meant being left on a cot to die, writhing in agony, until the Dullahan called out their name.

"The workhouses were as much end-of-life as the fever hospitals. More often than not, confinement in one refuge, led to their demise in another. Understandably, some of the poor preferred hunger to entering the multi-story damp factories of hard labor, in return for a few meager rations. That all changed with the Potato Famine.

"In a few short years, by mid-nineteenth century, there was no food, period! Despondent men, ashamed they could not provide for their families, wandered off into the hills or woods to die, just like an aging or sick animal. This at a time when Irish beef, milk and produce was being exported to Britain, and other nations of the Commonwealth. Protestant landowners were not about to share their harvest with their Catholic brethren, unless they extracted an exorbitant price.

"Fewer and fewer families had anything left to sell or barter. Unscrupulous merchants offered farthings instead of shillings for clothing or household furniture. 'Take it or leave it,' became their mantra.

"There have always been profiteers off the misery of others. Lawyers are notorious for it. There was no help from Britain, other than to open more workhouses. At the height of the famine, more than one-quarter of Ireland's sons and daughters populated workhouses.

"There were no stray dogs in Ireland. If a farmer was fortunate to own animals, they were soon sacrificed. In time, there was nothing left to kill or butcher. Family owned livestock was the first to go. Once eaten, there was no replacing the animal or what it produced. No eggs, milk or cheese. Few could hold on to a breeding pair. Farm animal auction prices were beyond the reach of most. Hens were last to go. Crowing roosters were relegated to folklore.

"A fungus attacked the potato crop, rendering the variety known as Lumpers into an inedible, black mush. The farmer did not understand the lack of diversity in the genetic makeup of the Lumper made it susceptible to disease. Digging up one blackened potato usually meant the entire field was lost. Can you imagine seeing that first potato?" George asked, directly.

"Every year they replanted Lumper potatoes, because their seeds were the cheapest. And each year they lost more of their crop. The potato was vital to the Irish economy. The vegetable could sustain a family throughout the year. Mixed with some milk, it provided the necessary vitamins and nutrients for a healthy diet, along with carbohydrates for energy. It wasn't gourmet dining, but it was palatable.

"Then one day they couldn't do that. By 1850, the entire potato harvest was destroyed. Within a few years there was mass starvation throughout the country. Only those who could afford to travel, were able avoid hunger."

"So why didn't they find a cure for the fungus, or switch to broccoli?" queried, Crash.

"You have to remember, this is happening almost a hundred years before penicillin is discovered," replied George. "It was a time when the industrial revolution was more focused on developing a better steam engine or a synthetic dye to color cotton red. Basic sterility practices were non-existent in hospitals, where sometimes more than half the patients died.

"It wasn't until the latter part of the century that vaccines were developed for smallpox, cholera, typhus, plague, and a host of other diseases that had been pandemic, wiping out entire populations. Such medical breakthroughs were not as profitable as time and research spent on manufacturing inventions. Whatever it is in life, it's always about the money," George concluded.

"In answer to your question about broccoli," George resumed, "that would have been a great substitute. It contains all the necessary vitamins and minerals, and can be cooked or eaten raw. The problem was, like so many other vegetables, the rocky native soil could not promote their growth. The climate hovers around fifty or sixty degrees, with overcast skies much of the time. Sometimes it seems like it rains every day. A lot of crops simply couldn't grow. But, the potato flourished, yielding twice the harvest of other crops.

"Unfortunately the type of potato planted was the Lumper, so called because they are irregular shaped with exterior lumps or knots. As I said, seeds were cheap, and it took root in all types of soil. The Lumper was a pure strain, and as such could not mutate to fight the disease that was causing it to rot. Incredibly, farmers sowed the same tainted ground each year with Lumpers. The crop's failure was a genetic problem. At the time, Gregor Mendel's work was in its infancy. His discoveries would come too late for those hit by the famine.

"Probably the solution was all around them, they just didn't realize it, believing the supply was infinite and the famine to be short lived. Surrounded by the Atlantic, Irish and Celtic Oceans, Ireland's seaweed rich coastline was a repository for all the vitamin, mineral and vital nutrient needs of man. Carrageen moss and dulse varieties sustained those living on Arranmore Island, off the coast of Donegal.

"Some species, if undercooked were not as well digested as others, resulting in dysentery, curtailing any further interest. And, rather than cultivate the shoreline crop, replanting after each harvest, people stripped beaches bare. Eventually tree bark was eaten, along with various weeds and unripened fruit.

"All too often, starved Irish deluded themselves into believing carrion could be ingested safely. Depending on the extent of decay and necrosis, the result was usually fatal. In less than five years, much of the population had starved to death. England did little to ease their suffering, despite having taxed their subjects for hundreds of years."

"You would think they learned something from the past, taxing the American Colonies until they were bled dry, giving nothing in return," Crash wondered aloud, affirming his belief in the importance of history.

"Unfortunately, the British government viewed the Irish as deserving of their fate due to a misconception they were lazy, and followed a false religion," offered George, before adding, "A callous belief that only the best survive among mankind, further justified their disdain."

Crash spoke up. "My family left County Meath, not too far from Dublin, right around 1850. Some took the direct route, a boat straight to Liverpool. You ate whatever you brought on board with you. It was never enough. Other Irish families went to Australia, no doubt wanting to get as far away from England as they could. Only those who could afford the fare were able to flee. Many passengers were contagious for cholera, some unknowing. So many died on these voyages, the vessels were referred to as coffin ships; bodies were unceremoniously tossed overboard.

"Many came to Canada and the United States, bringing with them the cholera epidemic, allowing it to take hold in North and South America. Those who survived, however, brought a work ethic, which gave them employment opportunities unheard of back home. More came. Their productivity and new found wealth eventually let them fuel Ireland's War of Independence. This much I learned from my grandfather," stated Crash, as George nodded knowingly.

CHAPTER SEVEN

COGADH NA SAOIRSE

The Irish War of Independence broke out in January, 1919. Guerrilla forces of the IRA fought the British over the issue of Home Rule. Treaty negotiations, led in part by Michael Collins, resulted in the Irish Free State or Irish Republic as it became known.

By 1921, with England still trying to recover economically from the Great War, a decision was made to offer the IRA a truce. It was the age old economic principle of "guns or butter." The pandemic Spanish Flu was in its waning days, leaving a worldwide death toll of almost 100 million. Fear of the influenza's return caused politicians to agree on more spending for medical research to find a cure or vaccine to prevent another outbreak. The timing of the truce offer couldn't have been better for the IRA. They were about to run out of guns, and long ago had run out of butter.

❧   ❧   ❧

As occasionally happens in the Los Angeles Basin, a torrent of rain curtailed any training plans. After viewing the track, George decided galloping over the sloppy surface might lead to injuries. The little gain in fitness was not worth a chance of injury. George may have been a risk taker while running messages for Collins, but he operated with an abundance of caution when it came to readying a horse for a race.

"You ready for some more war stories?" George asked his audience of one, morning chores now complete.

"Sure," answered Crash, eager to learn more.

"By the end of the Great War," started George, "England had lost a lot of men. Twenty thousand alone died on the first day of fighting at the Somme, in France. Most of these casualties were due to the British mandate that only Lords and Earls could be officers. These privileged gentry didn't know how to load their own guns on a pheasant shoot, much less possess any real battlefield skills.

"Consequently, young teenagers were ordered by the thousands to fix bayonets, climb out of the trenches and charge over barbed wire and minefields, only to be machine gunned or blown apart by Krupp Feldhaubitz howitzers, having a velocity of 1700 mph.

"In response to German gassing, the British ordered chlorine gas to be discharged into enemy lines. Unfortunately, the officers often-times failed to properly calculate wind direction, causing the gas to be ingested by their own men.

The painting *Over the Top,* a 1917 oil by John Nash, best depicts the officers' lack of skilled leadership. Of eighty men serving with the First Battalion Artists Rifles, almost all were killed or wounded in a matter of minutes, as they exited the safety of their trenches, when ordered to push toward the north of France.

"Impatient for independence and Home Rule, a faction within the IRA wanted war. 'The only way to start a war,' said one member, 'is to kill someone.' A few days later, two Royal Irish Constabulary officers were ambushed and shot dead. There would be 600 more RIC casualties in the first year of war.

"No love was lost between the people and the RIC. Their inception predated the famine. Remember, at that time no Catholics could serve on police forces and the RIC was responsible for enforcing evictions of tens of thousands of Catholics, their land confiscated by British protestants; a fact not overlooked by the constables' executioners.

"The war began in 1919. People boycotted the RIC, refusing to sell them food or dry goods. Constables resorted to taking food and supplies at gunpoint. The law quickly became lawless. RIC barracks and income tax offices were burned out. The court system collapsed.

"No one would come forward to serve as a juror. Police left the service in droves. With anarchy looming, the Irish Republican Police was formed to fill the void, until the Guardians of the Peace, or *Garda Siochána* was established in 1922.

"Although taxes were collected, they weren't paid over to Britain. Over five million dollars was contributed to the new Provisional Irish Republican government by Irish Americans, an astronomical amount for the time. The money enabled the new government to get a solid financial foothold.

"A general election was held, and the party of the Republic won an overwhelming majority. But, they did not take their seats within parliament in Britain. They set up their own parliament at home. Britain responded by dissolving the election and declaring martial law. With the jury system suspended, the military court-martialed civilians. Soon there was all out war.

"Any restraint by either side gave way to an 'eye for an eye' mindset. When the local IRA killed a soldier in one town, it often resulted in the British Army burning and looting the entire village. Retaliation was always ramped up.

"Shootings of women and children, round-ups of suspected insurgents, burning, looting, torture and rape became part of daily life. The Irish economy stagnated. Every commodity was in short supply, except hate."

"Wow, and you were in that?" asked Crash, amazed someone could experience such turmoil and live to tell about it.

"Yes," answered George. "As I said, I was in an Active Service Unit, under Michael Collins. He was big in stature and big in the movement. We all referred to him as the Big Fella. We mostly raided arms facilities, other units ambushed RIC patrols. I usually served as a courier between the Big Fella and different units, cells made up of seven or eight men.

"There was a mistrust that codes would be broken if wireless transmissions were used. Collins faithfully believed no imaginable torture could pry the information from any one of us, if we were captured; such was our dedication to the cause. Looking back, I was really just a kid, a few years older than you. It was a scary time."

A groom interrupted with a question about shipping. Responding, George changed the subject. "Del Mar starts next week, we need to pack the tack. I can't wait. Every year I close up my house in Coldwater Canyon and rent an apartment overlooking the ocean for the summer. I came here in the Twenties and can tell you the traffic and the smog haven't improved. Last week I had to drive out to Riverside to inspect a yearling for sale. The smog was so thick you couldn't see oncoming traffic, unless they turned on their headlights. When I got out, my eyes started burning. I sure didn't stay long. Living in Los Angeles for so long, I'm already having trouble breathing."

"You don't think it could be the Camels do you?" queried Crash, sincerely concerned for his friend's health.

George shook his head from side to side, shooting Crash an irritated glance, reiterating his denial.

"If we're leaving, may be I can cut out early tomorrow and drive down to Chino to visit Grace. Can we get the first horse to the track by six and finish by the break?"

"Sure thing, *compadre*," said George in a friendly tone, apparently having got past Crash's cigarette comment. Just don't tell the warden who I really am. I wouldn't want MI5 or Interpol picking me up," he said, half-kidding.

"You think?" questioned a doubtful Crash. "Not likely after forty years."

"I wouldn't bet on it," George answered in earnest. Right now, there are a lot of troubles in Ireland. Sometimes, you just never know who has it in for you. You make enemies and don't even realize it. Oblivious. Your enemies get into a position of power, then seek to exact vengeance.

"You can't be too careful. After the War, the IRA became fragmented, divided by differing philosophies on the partition of Northern Ireland. I've managed to stay under the radar this long, no sense in flying in front of it now. Best not to say too much. See you early in the morning, then."

The trip to Chino was fifty miles of surface streets through the LA suburb of Whittier, then onto State Route 60, where he passed by Hacienda Heights, then Diamond Bar, before arriving at the prison. Laid out like a college campus, Frontera is set on over one hundred acres. Only maximum and medium security level has a razor wire perimeter fence, with armed guards positioned in towers.

Having made the initial call to police and because of her acknowledgment of guilt in the plea, the Bureau of Prisons considered Grace a low flight risk, permitting her to serve her sentence in the unfenced minimum security area. Cells were more like dormitory rooms, instead of the caged quarters with steel bars in medium and maximum security. The focus was on reform, rather than punishment, despite the absence of toilet seats on the cold, stainless steel commodes. Most saw it for what it was, an effort by CIW to keep the despondent from picking up a made-to-order noose.

Grace appeared in an open visitors area with correction officers standing by. Crash soon got an earful. At the time of her arrest, officers discovered the sister was pregnant by her high school boyfriend. The uncle had intercourse with Grace's sibling on two recent occasions. And, her mother had pimped sis out to the landlord in exchange for rent. The mother was charged with child endangerment, child abuse, and felonious pandering of a minor. The landlord was charged with statutory rape and sexual assault of a minor. The engaging in prostitution charge was dropped.

Both adults were in LA County Jail awaiting trial. Scared and unwilling to testify, the sister was already into delinquent behavior. To the visiting caseworkers, the foster mother reported marijuana use and shoplifting as increasingly frequent. The three brothers were detained at MacLaren Hall, itself having a reputation for the physical and sexual abuse staff inflicted upon the children.

Unable to be placed in a suitable foster home, the boys ran away, joining up with the Crips in their old neighborhood. Eventually, two would side with the Piru Street faction, when it split with the rest of the Compton based Crips, to form the Bloods. Wearing rival colors of blue or red, the brothers were now destined to fight or kill each other in order to preserve their gangs' turf and control of the local drug trade.

Crash was shocked to hear all this, then paralyzed by what Grace revealed next.

"I have found comfort with another inmate," she stammered, explaining, "it's all about survival in here. Besides, I've been sent to a prison, not a convent."

Neither the simplicity of the racetrack, his middle school education at St. Aloysius Academy, nor growing up in a two parent family had prepared him to comprehend such lifestyles. He was an alien, descended into the netherworld.

The usually glib Crash could not find words to respond. On the drive down, he wondered if they would ever get back together. He was committed to help her get through the nightmare. By the time she was paroled, Grace would be twenty-six, with plenty of life to live. Now, he didn't know what to think; incapable of thought.

"What's your friend's name?" Crash asked,

trying to sound unperturbed.

"Janelle," Grace answered, curtly.

"Is that all? No last name?" asked Crash, unfamiliar with inmate protocol.

"How about number 24601?" she answered, with a smug grin.

"That's a big number. Are there that many in this prison?"

"It feels like it sometimes. Especially in the mess hall. Actually, I just borrowed that number from Jean Valjean," she laughed.

"What, you know *Les Miserables?*" Crash asked, in amazement.

"Got plenty of spare time. Might even read *War and Peace* before I get out," Grace smiled.

"You're too much," Crash said, affectionately. "So what's Janelle in for?"

"She was working as a housekeeper in ritzy Brentwood. Most people that live there don't know how to pump gas. Anyhow, Janelle told me she got caught stealing some silverware. When the cops searched her one room apartment, they found candlesticks, some high-end handbags, earrings and a necklace. Together they weren't worth more than $2000 and everything was returned.

"But, my friend is a poor White girl and not real bright. The D.A. saw a chance to pad his statistics. A slam-dunk for sure. He grouped some items and separated others to make up four felony grand theft charges and two misdemeanors. Burglary charges were also lumped on."

"What, she was the housekeeper!" exclaimed a surprised Crash.

"Yeah, but the District Attorney claimed she entered the premises for the purpose of stealing, not cleaning. She made it worse by talking to the cops without a lawyer. Told them she took the stuff over a five day period, so she got charged with five separate counts of burglary."

"That's insane," responded Crash, visibly upset. "Did she have any priors?"

"One, shoplifting some buttons from a Kresge Five & Ten, when she was a juvenile."

"Holy Cow! She got screwed over," stated Crash, surprised.

"Done all the time," said Grace, a hardness to her tone. "The only way a White broad, who wears Louis Vuitton, winds up in here is if they commit murder. They get a pass on nonviolent crime. You wouldn't believe the bullshit offenses some of these women are in for.

"Anyhow, the prosecutor added up the years for each crime and was gonna ask for thirty years. Consecutive terms for each offense. Had he recommended concurrent sentences, she would have only been looking at three years. Some guys are just pricks.

"So when her public defender urged her to take a plea deal she jumped at the chance. Her sentence is longer than mine. A rich white girl, who could afford a 'name' defense attorney, would have got probation and community service, since restitution wasn't an issue. With luck, she would be assigned to the Junior League, making phone calls for a clothing drive. Any other schmuck would have to scrub toilets for Parks and Recreation. Like Victor Hugo writes, 'there is no justice for the poor.'

"The guard is tapping her watch. I better get back to the cell block. Come see me again. Please," she pleaded

"Be sure to," Crash promised, adding, "I'll put something in your canteen account on my way out."

He was relieved when a khaki uniformed officer approached, announcing time was up. Muscular and stocky, her profile resembled wrestling's erstwhile villain, Freddie Blassie. Gazing around the room, it was apparent other inmates, and some guards, preferred women. Feeling compassion for all Grace had been through, he took her hand and gave it a gentle squeeze good-bye.

Returning to her cell, Grace climbed onto the top bunk, scared for herself and for Crash. She closed her eyes and thought of her first night in that bunk. At ten p.m., lights were ordered out, darkness obscured reality. If she tried hard enough, she could pretend she was away at college, ascribing the incessant chatter to her sorority's slumber party. Lying there, so alone, afraid of how she would be able to cope with prison life, how the harshness of it all would change her, she had sought solace by pleasuring herself.

Quietly, she increased the circular motion of her forefinger until she was removed from her surroundings, unaware her celly was standing alongside. She felt Janelle's warm touch against her cheek, the heat of her very presence, moments before Janelle leaned toward her with a kiss. At first she resisted, but the loneliness of the moment overcame her, permitting her to succumb to Janelle's advances.

Soon their fingers joined, adding to Grace's stimulation. Whatever barriers existed, quickly gave way to a rush, unlike any she experienced before. Unsure if the sensations were brought on by crossing the line of a taboo, or a genuine attraction to her own gender, Grace was sure of one thing. As long as Janelle was incarcerated, loneliness would be an abstract concept, not to be felt again.

On the drive back to Hollywood Park, Crash kept thinking how quickly their lives had come apart. Grace's life had all but disintegrated. He could not erase visions of Grace and Janelle together. He hoped it wasn't a permanent conversion. Frontera was more like Sapphist Eden, except instead of wearing a sarong and gardenia in her hair, Sappho wore a grey jump-suit, imprinted with CIW. He was confident Grace would get through it, just not so sure how she would come out on the other side. Earlier in their relationship, she had warned Crash she carried baggage. What may have once been carry-on, now required a hand truck.

The next morning, he sauntered down the shedrow, head down, with both hands in his pockets. Mumbling hello, he helped George put protective cotton bandages on the horses, before boarding the 18-wheeler, emblazoned with the red and black colors of Turf Line Express, lettered on the polished aluminum sides.

"Del Mar is opening next week. You are coming, aren't you?" questioned George, not sure how any mood change may affect his exercise boy's plans.

"Yes, I'm still going," he said, sounding depressed.

"You look like you've lost your best friend."

"Maybe not my 'best,' but a friend, yes," Crash said, as he recounted his visit for George, giving updates on Grace's family.

"Good God, Man! Where did you meet such a woman?" he questioned, with dramatic flair.

"In a bar," came the honest reply.

"Take it from someone whose been married five times. Stay away. She's poison. Pull you right down with her, she will."

"Not sure if I can. And what kind of friend am I, if I cut her off?" his question tinged with guilt.

"Well, my boy, at least you will have a few years to give it some thought," he chuckled; the attempt at humor unappreciated.

CHAPTER EIGHT

MICHEÁL Ó COILEÁIN

"Tell me more about that guy you called Big Fella," Crash begged, in his quest to learn all he could of Irish history.

Replying, George began, "Michael Collins was the head of intelligence for the IRA, then chairman of the Provisional Government. He is as revered in Ireland as George Washington is in America. He was a founder of today's Ireland. He was smart, having worked for brokerage firms in London and New York, before returning to join the Irish Republican Brotherhood, later becoming its president.

"He was brave, fighting at the Easter Rising, and then imprisoned. Although he fought along-side Pádraig Pearse, he disagreed with his plan to occupy the General Post Office, believing it to be indefensible, once British reinforcements were deployed; likening their position to The Alamo.

"Michael had plenty of military savvy, even though he lacked the formal training of a Sandhurst or West Point graduate. When it came to calculating the opposition forces, either British or Anti-treaty IRA, he showed an innate skill. The man was born take charge. Sadly, he underestimated the animosity of those he fought for," said the admiring member of Michael's army unit, reflecting on those volatile times.

"Collins emerged as a leader in the reborn *Sinn Féin* party. During the War of Independence, he utilized 'flying columns' as a guerrilla warfare tactic to compensate for being out-manned. Like the Plains Indians, he would launch an attack, then immediately retreat, keeping casualties to a minimum. It was a tactic roving Indian bands employed, whenever encountering a wagon train or cavalry troop exceeding their number. I learned that from the movies," George winked, as he spoke.

Paramilitary forces were established by Britain to combat the IRA's guerrilla warfare. The Black and Tans and the Auxiliary Division were made up of borderline criminals. Violent and brutal in their conduct, they became effective assassins, a tactic both sides excelled in.

On a quiet Sunday morning, when most horses are handwalked, George called out for Crash to join him on a bale of hay. "Have a seat," he said, patting some first cutting timothy, grown in Washington's Yakima Valley. "Best you can buy in the Northwest," he remarked. "On an ordinary Dublin Sunday like this," he began, "with people headed off to mass or a picnic to watch the soccer match, all hell broke loose.

"Unlike Pádraig Pearse, Michael wanted to avoid the bloodshed of his followers, whenever possible, having tried to dissuade Pearse from his 'blood sacrifice' at the GPO. He was not so concerned with the bloodletting of Brits. In fact, he formed an assassination unit called 'The Squad' specifically to kill British agents and to curtail spying from within the IRA. Unfortunately, this led to Bloody Sunday.

"In response to intelligence that loyalist paramilitary groups were planning to assassinate leading Republicans, Michael Collins, then head of the IRA, gave the order to execute some fifty British and Irish paid informers. The list included a bunch of roughnecks known as the Cairo gang.

"Centered around Dublin, their specific locations were revealed to the IRA Death Squads by housemaids, deliverymen and those sympathetic to the cause within the Royal Constabulary. Coordinated assassinations commenced early on a Sunday morning.

"At exactly 9:00 a.m., two IRA, wearing tweed overcoats and flat caps tipped toward their brow, entered Mrs. MacGillycuddy's kip off Dorset Street, on Dublin's north side, not far from the River Liffey. A stones throw from Croke Park, the building itself was once a shop, the front windows having been bricked in to make extra bedrooms.

"Guests were received in the parlour, adjacent to a small kitchen and a room with a bathtub and toilet. Beneath the staircase, a door marked *Fir*, opened to a cramped space with barely enough room for the urinal. Above it, a directive for the British clientele cautioned, 'No French Letters,' next to an arrow pointing downward to the basin.

"Upstairs, three more rooms accommodated those whose services were most often requested. Dormers, called the 'last chance' rooms, by Mrs. Mac, extended out from the rooftop, providing space for the disobedient or diseased.

"Failing to get along, either unable or unwilling to please, was a sure ticket to a Magdalene House. Chimney's on either end of the red brick and mortar, took the chill off the rooms. Mrs. MacGillycuddy was ever mindful of customer comfort; undressed in the cold, they were not likely to leave satisfied."

ఈ ఈ ఈ

Named for the biblical prostitute who washed the feet of Jesus, the Magdalene Asylums were a variation on the workhouses. They began in mid-1700's England as a refuge for Protestant women, who practiced the world's oldest profession. In Ireland, these institutions were first run by the Church of Ireland and Presbyterians. By the beginning of the 1800s, the Catholic Church saw where under the guise of redemption, the collection plate could derive a benefit from the girl's services. Once again, the unchaste were to be exploited and abused, now within the confines of the asylums, rather than kips.

The moral standard of the time required a bride to bring her virginity to the alter. Premarital sex was unthinkable. After all, that is what the kips were for. This double standard resulted in many of the "fallen" turning to the Sisters of Magdalene. Whether the women sinned for money or love, it was all the same. Once they gave it up, they could only be saved by prayer and hard labor. The Magdalene mantra was *Do Penance or Perish.*

While in these institutions, some girls gave birth, having entered after they conceived. Others brought their children with them. Except for the infants, all worked. Many of the children were adopted out, the unlucky ones enslaved by their benefactors. Every child was indelibly marked by the immorality of their mother. What began as a refuge for women in desperate need of food, shelter and safety became a prison. Ireland's own moral compass could no longer find North. Fathers who may have paid for alley sex behind a pub or the local kip, were all too quick to sign a disgraced daughter into a Magdalene House. Their long term confinement was assured, as most families steadfastly refused to allow the wayward member to return.

In time, the asylums grew to be a major business, thriving financially within all the larger cities. Their product? Laundry. Essentially they cornered the clean linen market for hospitals, hotels, military barracks, and any other business that relied on clean towels and pillows. Not surprisingly, this included the kips. No other laundry could compete against an enterprise which paid its help with a few meals a day.

Once inside the Magdalene Houses many women became institutionalized, completely dependent on the good sisters for sustenance and salvation. Few returned to society unscathed. The Magdalene Laundries were just another English thorn in the side of Irish culture. It was not until the end of The Troubles, as Ireland moved into the twenty-first century, that the last of the these medieval asylums were closed.

❧ ❧ ❧

"The Republicans saw Mrs. Mac's as a poignant reminder of Ireland's subservience to British rule," George continued.

"Otherwise good Catholic girls, whose impoverished families relied on them for their existence, were exploited by the occupying army of their Imperial rulers. The IRA carried resentment and Tommy guns, as they ascended the stairs. Kicking open the door to room six, a frightened teenager from County Clare, jumped up, dressed only in cut-away, frilled nickers.

'Och, I'll be on my way,' said the redhead," her fear mimicked by George.

"A normally stoic, former British colonel, now in command of a division of Black and Tans, huddled naked before them. Sweat pooled at the roots of his nicotine stained, ginger moustache.

His flaccid member, 'at ease.' Tasting salt, the colonel whimpered a plea for his life, as soon as the American-made .45 caliber Thompsons were leveled at him, intent on shredding his English soul.

"Not that native Dubliners didn't patronize the kips, but they were just as likely to have lost their land, livelihood, and loved ones to the British. At the very least, it gave them a resentment in common with the girls, besides a shared hope for Ireland to be free."

Continuing with the story, George resorted to playing a change in characters, a talent he developed at the Abbey Theater.

"Boyo, did you pay the lass yet?" asked one of the men.

Shaking his head, "no," the colonel was chastised for sinning against God and compromising the virtue of the poor and uneducated, "a class 'your kind' created," said the gunman, wagging his finger. Next, the colonel was asked for permission to access his trouser pockets, hanging on a peg with his uniform.

"Certainly," came a hastened reply, the added time and courtesy giving the colonel false hope.

Motioning to the redhead, one of the gunmen politely told her to empty the colonel's pockets, before she left. In a reassuring tone, he was told any change would be left with Mrs. Mac on account for his next visit, if he was still so inclined, after having just been admonished.

The visibly relieved patron stood, holding a

pillow over his privates, promising never to
return, asking to put his uniform back on. One
of the men nodded his assent, saying it was a
military courtesy, 'one soldier to another,' to
spare him any indignity.

The latter comment caused the officer renewed consternation, asking himself if they
were referring to him being found dead naked
or, preferably, being ushered out unclothed. He
was willing to submit to any humiliation, which
might prolong his life.

'I suppose you have a wife and children in
England?' queried the less menacing of the pair,
with seemingly kind interest.

'As a matter of fact I do. In Brighton,' he
responded, once again hopeful he would live to
enjoy their love and feel their embrace.

Whether it was the clatter of the junk man
selling his wares from the side of his horse drawn
cart along the street below, or the incessant
honking of motor cars on Dorset, their drivers
late for nine o'clock mass, the colonel failed to
hear the Dullahan call his name.

Donning his smartly pressed khaki tunic, the
colonel buttoned his jacket, leaving his Sam
Browne belt and pistol on a peg, in deference
to the odds of two against one. Next came the
toughest question of them all. Presumptively, he
reached for his dark green, almost black beret.
Putting an end to the cat and mouse game, he
addressed the less menacing one.

'I beg your pardon, Sir, may I have permission

to leave, Sir?' Nervously, he awaited a reply. The rat-a-tat-tat from a Tommy gun denied his request.

৶   ৶   ৶

Shifting gears, George proceeded: "Simultaneously breaking down the doors at eight other locations, Collins' death squads killed thirteen men, along with a number of wounded. Among the dead were several MI5 secret service and Auxiliaries. In a speech addressing the necessity of the killings, Collins stated, '... they have destroyed without trial. I have paid them back in their own coin.'

A retaliatory response followed that very afternoon. Black and Tans combined with Auxiliaries and local RIC formed a lethal force targeting civilians. Leyland lorries transported them in a convoy to Croke Park, where Dublin was scheduled for a football match with Tipperary. Intent on inflicting retribution upon unarmed innocents, the loyalist's Red Right Hand pummelled spectators.

A Vickers machine gun, mounted atop a Rolls Royce armored car, met those fleeing the stadium. The death toll of fourteen people included two, who were trampled to death. Michael Hogan, an acclaimed soccer player, was among the dead, along with women and children. Seventy others were wounded, victims of indiscriminate shooting. There were no casualties on the side of the perpetrators.

Officially, the shootings were condemned as an

unauthorized use of force, owing in part to international outcry. Unofficially, the attacks were condoned as a necessary response to the Sunday morning assassinations. By nightfall, the RIC captured three IRA officers, who took part in planning the attacks on MI5 and Auxiliaries. They were tortured, then murdered without trial.

Public opinion in England supported the Croke Park massacre. The Irish, however, were unforgiving, increasing their support for the Republican Party, solidifying their determination to become independent.

By 1920, there was a 10,000 guineas bounty on Michael's head. In December of that same year, the IRA twice ambushed Auxiliary patrols in County Cork. Seventeen Auxiliaries were killed in the first skirmish. The British responded by imposing martial law.

Following a pattern, the IRA attacked another patrol, using an IRA member dressed as a British officer for a decoy, stopping two lorries loaded with Auxiliaries. The attack resulted in one dead and more than a dozen wounded. The IRA escaped unharmed.

Enraged at being tricked by the charade, the remaining able bodied Auxiliaries went into a local pub and dragged the young men outside, into the street, regardless of any IRA affiliation. Stripped naked and badly beaten, they were made to sing 'God Save the King,' until they dropped to the roadway, unconscious.

Not yet satisfied, a few nights later, armed

Auxiliaries accompanied by British soldiers carrying petrol bombs stormed the City Center of Cork. Over five acres of the city's buildings were ravaged by fire, in addition to more than forty businesses and three hundred residences. Bullets prevented firemen from doing their job. There were numerous civilian injuries and a few deaths. The conflagration rendered more than two thousand homeless. A similar number were left jobless."

"Good Lord, George, how did people cope?" Crash asked, astonishment in his eyes. He could not comprehend the cruelty Britain's soldiers inflicted upon their citizens. No wonder they revolted, he thought.

"Novenas and rosaries helped," answered George. "Hate escalated. Throughout Ireland, those who opposed the British loathed them. The animosity became personal, not just political."

"What about your bounty? Did Collins die? He couldn't have been much older than you."

"True, but there are no mortality tables in war. He was betrayed by an Irish bullet. As to my bounty, I'm sure it was a lot less. Most of the time, those Tans put up wanted posters with a reward of twenty pounds. Believe me, you could get turned in for that sum. To put that amount in perspective, the fare to book passage to America was ten pounds, three pounds for steerage. I can't remember exactly how much was on my head, but I couldn't wait to 'get outta Dodge,' as they say in Western movies."

Changing the subject, he stated, "The track just announced the break is over. I've got one more. Take him an easy mile," instructed George. Working for this man, Crash was getting an education unlike any available at a university. And, tuition was free.

"You see that hill up there?" he asked, pointing Crash to the north side of the track. "That's the town of Solano Beach. I'm going to find a small cottage there and retire. Got my Coldwater Canyon house up for sale. I've already retired once, from motion pictures, now it's time to leave the horses. I don't breathe so good, and the dust on the backstretch can't help. Too much smog in LA.

"The air here will be easier to breathe, fanned by a sea breeze. I'll just kick back and enjoy the ocean views. I can hang out with a few Hollywood friends during Del Mar's racing season. You are always welcome to visit though," George said, reassuringly.

"I'll be sure to. Will you have anything to run here next year?"

"Just one or two. I've already sold my brood-mares. They were a mistake. I should never have read Federico Tesio on horse breeding. He made raising champions look easy. A genius. He about broke guys like me, who thought he was just a simple Italian farmer.

"If he can do it, so can anyone. At least that's what everybody thought. Maybe he left out a key chapter. Anyway, no one's been able to duplicate his success. The bloodlines he established re-invented the racehorse. He gave us Nearco and Ribot, and they in turn begot Northern Dancer and Graustark. Tesio's influence is worldwide, has been for almost half a century."

"Man, you have had an exciting life!"

"I dunno about that. You don't want life to be too exciting. Why don't we run up Jimmy Durante Boulevard to Denny's. Maybe I'll tell you more about the Big Fella."

"I'd like that," said Crash, getting into George's right hand drive, silver Bentley Sports Saloon. The morning sun glistened off the lacquer finish, as George steered toward an isolated parking area to avoid door dings and onlookers.

"Is this posh or what?" marveled Crash, sitting on genuine leather seats, surrounded by burled, Italian walnut.

"Acquired in extravagant times, lad," informed George, as he resumed the previous day's story.

"Collins set about organizing the Irish Republican Army. He consolidated the loosely knit, varied assortment of guerrilla units that sprung up in the thirty or so counties of Ireland, weaving them together with the common thread of making Ireland free. Separate units had wreaked havoc on the RIC, but they lacked direction. There was no momentum, until Michael channeled their courage into a well disciplined, armed force.

"Some military historians have called Collins the founder of guerrilla warfare. Once the newly formed army was established, funding and munitions flowed from Irish America. Around this same time, a guy named Éamon deValera led *Sinn Féin*."

"What's Irish about deValera?"

"Not the name itself, Kid. That came from his father's Spanish heritage. He was from Cuba. His mother was Irish, but deValera himself was born in New York. A fortuitous event, if there ever was one."

"How so?" the inquisitive listener interrupted.

"As I was about to say, somewhere between the Easter Rising and the War of Independence, British agents arrested him for treason. Twice mind you. A year after the Rising he was granted amnesty, only to be re-arrested the following year. He would have been executed, but because he was born in America, Britain spared his life, sentencing him instead to a lifetime confinement in an old, damp castle; no doubt a death sentence in disguise. The United States had been a critical ally to Britain, during the just concluded Great War. Under the circumstances, hanging deValera would have touched off a diplomatic firestorm.

"This was the same rationale that kept him from the gallows after the Rising. Stateside, it would have had political repercussions for Woodrow Wilson's presidency. His Democratic party won the election with the help of New York's notoriously corrupt Tammany Hall, a well-oiled vote getting machine, supported by Irish immigrants.

"Accompanied by Harry Boland, none other than Michael Collins helped deValera gain freedom in a daring escape from Lincoln Prison, a veritable fortress in the north of England. Boland was a member of the Irish Volunteers, and very close to Collins. So close, they were bound in a love triangle with Kitty Kiernan, as both men vied for her affections.

"Harry was very athletic, an accomplished hurler, dapper dresser, suave, and handsome, with a forget-me-not smile. Kitty found herself unable to let go. Harry may have been what you young people call a chick magnet, but above all, Harry was dedicated to the cause of a free Ireland, having fought at the Easter Rising.

"Michael was his equal in the good looks department; his strong face ruggedly crafted, as if sculpted by Rodin. Michael's engaging personality, winsome at times, was often tempered by his firebrand passion for a free Ireland. The precision in which the Lincoln Prison break was carried out, had the Big Fella's mark, undoubtedly moving him to the top of MI5's list of most wanted. Afterward, the men made their way to Liverpool, some 75 miles south, a considerable distance for the time."

"Did you know Kitty? What was she like?" Crash broke in, unintentionally interrupting the flow.

"Full of life. To look at, she was stunning. Classic features. First time I met her was when I stopped in the family bakery. They had the best

SHERGAR

cream pies in Dublin," George said, wistfully.

"Kitty always dressed to the nines. All style. Smart too. Could have made it in Hollywood. Like my second wife, Ruth Chatterton, Kitty had a sexy allure about her. Very pleasant, but a tragic figure, in a way."

"How's that?" asked his curious listener.

"The family was cursed with a hereditary kidney disease, chronic nephritis, known then as Bright's disease. Today it would be treated with antibiotics and dialysis, and those stricken could live a somewhat normal life. Back then, blood letting and laxatives were the only prescribed remedies to combat the illness.

"When Kitty was fifteen, her one sister died. The next year, another sister was struck down. The next year she lost both her parents. Ironically, her father was an undertaker. How horrid to be in that business and bury your own children, then your wife, knowing your turn might be next. The Irish lived with death. But, you never get used to burying your children. It can drive you stark raving mad.

"Kitty had a big heart, big enough for two men. You are young, but believe me, when I say you can be absolutely in love with two people at the same time. If it ever happens, you are tormented. She became engaged to Collins, having to choose between the men she loved, when he proposed.

"Before the wedding, he was assassinated by one of his own. It was years before she could put herself back together, eventually marrying and having a son, a godsend, born free of the family curse. Soon after he was born, she lost her brother, and a few years later, her surviving sisters. All to nephritis. Then, the Irish herald of death, the Dullahan, came calling on her at age fifty."

"God, George that's a terrible story. It couldn't be any sadder," said Crash, sincerely sympathetic for someone who had passed away many years ago. "She had to be strong woman."

"Aye, that she was," spoke George, allowing a slight brogue to enter the conversation. "Sorry, I got a little sidetracked," he added, apologizing for the digression.

"No, no, I want to hear it all," Crash responded.

"Once in Liverpool, deValera boarded a ship sailing to New York," George continued, picking up from where he left off, "while Michael and Harry returned to Ireland. The well educated deValera, who became a mathematics professor, continued to fight for the cause. His exceptional oratory skill and fund raising abilities served to bolster the treasury of *Sinn Féin* and the IRA. Later, in New York, he was joined in this effort by his good friend, Harry Boland, who soon returned for the elections as a member of *Sinn Féin*, winning the vote as representative of Roscommon.

"In a concession from Britain, deValera was able to return to Ireland after Independence, although he disagreed with partitioning the North, becoming a part of the anti-Treaty movement. Harry held the same view, both men sharing an important philosophical difference with Michael Collins. Where the beauty of a woman couldn't break apart his friendship with Harry, the baseness of politics succeeded. Each drew a line in the sand. Little did they know, they would both be killed for it."

"Go on," implored Crash.

"The treaty allowed the predominantly protestant Six Counties that made up Northern Ireland to opt out, remaining under British Rule. The rest of Ireland would become a Dominion, with its own parliament, the King to appoint the equivalent of a governor-general, similar to the Dominions of Canada and Australia.

"The members of parliament of the newly formed Irish Free State would take an oath of allegiance to the new constitution, requiring they be faithful to the King. Also, they would share Britain's public debt, give up strategic ports to the British, and support England in time of war.

"Ireland had stayed neutral throughout the Great War, a position most Britons found objectionable, some equating it with cowardice. Editorial cartoons of the day portrayed young Irish men holding a white feather.

"A vote to withdraw from Dublin rule would result in redrawing the northern border. Collins believed this provision compromised the economic integrity of Northern Ireland to stand alone. He thought this would sway the vote against opting out, resulting in a unified free Ireland. He was mistaken.

"Miscalculating the vote, Collins supported the treaty terms, believing it was the best that could obtained at the time. His friends, Boland and deValera were vehemently opposed, finding the notion of partition or a veiled oath to the crown, unacceptable, notwithstanding Collins' opinion the vote to partition would not pass.

"The signing of the truce and subsequent treaty ratification were the ingredients for a civil war, polarizing Ireland. Anti-treaty opponents and Pro-treaty advocates within *Sinn Féin* split the party. IRA members were similarly divided. All hell was about to break loose.

"Of course, I sided with Collins. He realized the war could not continue. The IRA was running on empty. If they had anything left, the IRA would have bargained better terms. To his credit, Michael recognized his lack of resources: arms and manpower were exhausted. He was David, going up against Goliath. Had he persevered, and Britain prevailed, the British would have crushed everything Irish, perhaps even their will to be free.

"Michael was in a no-win situation and he knew it. He believed the accord gave the Irish people 'the freedom to achieve freedom.' Upon affixing his signature to the treaty agreement, he commented, 'I may have signed my own death warrant.'

"Unbeknown to those angered at Michael, he

was secretly planning guerrilla warfare in the North, hoping to dislodge England from Ireland forever. Lacking support, and with the country on the brink of civil war, these plans were abandoned."

"You must have felt like you were on a roller coaster ride," interjected Crash.

"Higher than the one at Six Flags," confirmed George. "The vote to opt out by the Six Counties not only partitioned the North from the homeland, it was also the match that ignited the cannons of war."

"So what ever happened to Collins?" an inquisitive Crash asked.

"I was getting to that. Collins was Chairman of the post treaty Provisional Government, but gave up that position to become Commander-in-Chief of the National Army, made up of Pro-treaty IRA. Collins asserted the Republican Army, comprised of Anti-treaty IRA, must accept the Peoples vote to ratify the Treaty and accordingly lay down their arms. Toward this goal, he traveled to Cork, to meet with Anti-treaty IRA.

"Although the countryside was in the hands of Anti-treaty armed men, Collins declined basic security measures. He refused to believe he was in danger from those he had previously led in the IRA, even more so, while in his home county of Cork. Riding in an open car, he was a sitting duck.

"When his group was ambushed, he ordered them to return the fire, rather than drive out of range. He was as brazen as he was brave. Once he was hit, the attackers scattered, having assassinated a champion of a free Ireland.

"Over 500,000 attended his funeral in Dublin, where he lay in state for three days. Mourners lined the streets for six miles as the three mile long funeral cortege proceeded to Glasnevin, where his friend Harry Boland had been buried a few weeks before.

"Thousands of men and women, common laborers alongside professionals, clerks and clergy, walked behind a six-horse drawn caisson carrying Michael's casket, cloaked with the Irish Tricolor. A single white lily lay upon the coffin, placed there by Kitty Kiernan.

"No less than seventeen bands played Handel's 'Dead March.' Black crepe bunting surrounded lorries carrying hundreds of flowered wreaths to the gravesite. At Glasnevin, Irish bagpipes keened 'The Minstrel Boy.' It was a sad time for Ireland."

"I can't believe so many good men were either assassinated or executed. To lead, was a one way ticket to Glasnevin," Crash suggested.

"Understand, all war is depraved, but civil war is barbaric," George responded.

"Harry Boland fought shoulder to shoulder next to his friend Michael Collins, during the War of Independence, but joined forces with the Anti-treaty IRA. A few weeks before Michael was shot, Harry was gunned down in cold blood, unarmed, inside his hotel room, by Pro-treaty

IRA. I always wondered if Michael's death was simply retaliatory, rather than political. For sure, Michael never ordered the hit on Harry, despite any differences. He was loyal to his friends.

"Coincidence or not, the war was only going to get crazier. I used to worry that someone in the Black and Tans or Auxiliaries would arrest me. Convinced I was fair game for the British Army or MI5, I figured they might grab me.

"Then, suddenly, I had Anti-treaty IRA looking for me. It was only a matter of time, before some former comrade turned me in for the reward. Too many enemies, none of whom I had ever harmed, most I'd never seen. I was on the next boat to New York."

"How did it feel to be free from all that?" asked Crash.

"I never felt really free. I was glad to be out of the chaos, pleased I wasn't headed for a trip to Glasnevin, like so many I knew. But, I also felt guilty about leaving. And, I was constantly nervous, whenever a stranger approached; taking window seats only, at restaurants. After a few films, I was finally able to let my guard down and relax a little."

Switching back to the story, George resumed, "For all his military skill, Collins was also a statesman. Taking his duties seriously, he often brooded over his decisions, and how they would affect Ireland's pursuit of freedom. He was appointed to several important ministerial positions within the provisional government, filling in for deValera, when he was out of the country, even though the two men disagreed militarily and on governance. Collins wanted to wage a guerrilla style war to gain independence, raids and ambushes, utilizing his flying columns, and targeted assassinations.

"DeValera wanted to wage a conventional war, with uniformed soldiers marching in formation, and holding onto areas at all costs, once British forces were driven back. He believed it would give them greater credibility, leading to quicker recognition of the new republic by other nations. Collins, on the other hand, realized he was completely outnumbered and out-gunned. His recruits had little training and lacked the strict discipline of the British Army. A third approach was that proposed by Cathal Brugha.

"Brugha, who fought alongside Michael at the Easter Rising, had wanted to shift the War of Independence to the English mainland, keeping destruction and civilian casualties out of Ireland. Michael rejected this notion as it lacked feasibility and any chance of success.

"An elected representative of the *Sinn Féin* party, Brugha, also argued against ratifying the Treaty, in the Irish Parliament debates. When Civil War broke out, he commanded a small regiment of Anti-treaty forces, until a Pro-treaty bullet severed his femoral artery.

"Whether or not the populace agreed with their politics, they respected the sacrifices Ireland's leaders made on their behalf. Once again, thousands lined the streets of Dublin to pay homage, as Cathal Brugha's funeral procession made its way to Glasnevin.

"When the War of Independence truce was agreed to, the Anti-treaty deValera and Pro-treaty Collins found out just how divergent their political views were. DeValera was one of few Irish leaders of the time to survive. Always at the forefront of Irish politics, he was re-elected President of Ireland at age 84, for a second term, about the time you and I first met."

Refilling their coffee, the waitress left the bill. "Ham and eggs, a buck-ninety. Judas Priest!" exclaimed George. "I can remember when it was under four bits, including the coffee."

"C'mon George, you're showing your age. I've got to get goin'. Time to do a little body surfing," Crash declared proudly, getting up to leave.

"Watch out for sharks," advised George.

"Hey, there are more sharks on the racetrack than in the Pacific," his friend asserted.

CHAPTER NINE

PRINCESS MARGARET

The next morning Crash showed up, meeting Alex Maese at the barn. George wanted to work the grey filly in company with an older gelding, a multiple stakes winner with a proven track record. Asking Crash to breeze the filly, he assigned Alex the mount on Tinquilco. Although contemplating riding Alex on the grey in her racing debut, George had not yet made a decision, deeming it best for Alex not to know of her ability first hand.

In two previous years, Alex had won back-to-back Del Mar Futurities. His agent would pester George for the mount, if he learned she had talent. George instructed both riders to keep their horses together, breezing the 5/8ths as a team.

"Keep a hold of her," he said to Crash, "turn her loose that last forty yards, then let her gallop out around the turn."

Crash followed orders like a soldier. The filly flew by the Chilean bred, Tinquilco, getting the furlong past the wire in a solid :13 seconds. Time for the 5/8ths was a swift :59 4/5^{ths} seconds. The gallop-out was huge. Not surprisingly, Alex had a lot of questions, most of which were met with disinformation.

Crash could see what was going on. George wanted to get his filly racing fit, at the same time keeping her talent hidden. An infection had kept her out of action for much of Hollywood Park. Now, she was back, good as ever.

After Alex left for another barn, George turned to Crash, "So?" he questioned.

"Sooo, she is a running fool!" Crash answered emphatically. "Sure could have blown by the old stakester anytime I wanted to, like he was tied to a pole."

"Good thing you didn't. Soon as those clockers see speed, they start calling the gamblers, who pay them for inside information. She should be ready for her debut in another week. Don't go talking her up. We'll get better odds if word doesn't get out.

"Besides, I bred her. Foaled her myself, in the middle of the night. Paid the vet bills, the stud fee, broke her, on top of feeding her for more than two years, not knowing whether she could run, until this morning. It doesn't make sense to go touting her and have some high roller with no blood, sweat or capital invested, hammer her down at the mutuel windows."

"Agreed," said Crash, "no need to worry about me. I don't even know her name. Just don't talk in your sleep and no one will know a thing," he laughed.

After training hours, Crash went into his room and counted his stash. Living from paycheck to paycheck and betting on a few also-rans, he had managed to put aside only eighty dollars. With his next payday, he could up that by two hundred. When the time came, he would go all in.

Only one horse was scheduled to train the following Tuesday morning. "C'mon," said George, "You ready to go to work? I need you to jog the grey filly the wrong way."

Acknowledging his request, Crash grabbed a saddle and bridle and hung it on the saddle rack outside the filly's stall. The groom was inside ready to brush her off. Ignoring caution, Crash ducked under the stall webbing stretched across the entrance. The filly reacted when he stood up, letting out a squeal as she wheeled around the stall, causing both men to dive out into the shedrow.

"What the fuck?" hollered George, invoking an expletive he seldom used.

After Crash explained, he had to endure the mandatory lecture on safety first, reminding him of the ever present danger with a racehorse on tilt.

"And if you don't care about yourself, how about the horse? God help us if she got hurt," George sputtered, running out of steam, as he cooled down.

"Sorry, boss. I should have unsnapped the webbing and walked in. I'll tack her up, right away." Crash busied himself, making sure he stayed out of the way. He couldn't wait to get a leg up and trot off to the track.

While at Del Mar, he had no time to visit Grace, now more than a hundred miles away. His Buick had started to knock. Feeling a mixture of emotions: guilt, sympathy, love and anger, he wrote her each week about the horses he was galloping. Surely he could of done more to deter her from shooting the uncle, he thought. The internal dialogue continued, questioning whether isolation, fear, loss of family and friends, played a part in her finding comfort with another woman. Of course, came the reply.

Later, Crash learned the filly's name was Princess Margaret, prompting him to question George.

"How does someone fight for the IRA, then name a racehorse after the Queen's sister?"

George laughed, explaining, "a friend has a little girl, Margaret, and she is a real princess, I can assure you. Anyhow, you've probably seen the filly is in Saturday's entries, a maiden race going five-and-a-half furlongs. I named Alex on her. His agent will probably come by with a hundred questions. Do us both a favor and dummy up."

"Sure, glad to oblige."

Saturday morning, Crash took his paycheck to the cashier at the kitchen, buying five days of meal tickets. For insurance, he told himself. At the mutuel windows, he would go all in. He then sat down next to someone reading that day's edition of the *Racing Form*.

"Can I take a look at the past performances for the second race?" he asked the horseplayer seated alongside.

"Sure, let me know if you see something you like," replied the well-dressed patron, the barter cloaked in a cloud of innocence.

After perusing the running lines of each entrant, Crash assessed Princess Margaret's chances. She was in a good spot, having drawn post position number 5. More importantly, she would be overlooked in the betting. Her breeding was not so much obscure as it did not spell speed, critical at the short distance. In the workout with Tinquilco, she demonstrated enough quickness, coupled with the ability to track the leader, before accelerating.

Outside of Hollywood, George was an unknown, and even that limelight had faded. A deep riding colony boasted of 1943 Triple Crown winner, Johnny Longden, nicknamed "The Pumper," who was still going strong at fifty-seven, along with no less than nine others, all of whom had won major classics, including the Kentucky Derby. Bill Hartack, Willie Shoemaker, Johnny Sellers, Ray York, Braulio Baeza, Milo Valenzuela, and Hank Moreno, together, left little room for another jockey to pick up mounts. In a race with such icons of the turf, the presence of the underrated Alex Maese was sure to be disregarded.

Returning the *Racing Form*, Crash mentioned the One horse, "breaking from the rail, she should show speed. She will be in front, just don't know for how long."

The man appeared satisfied. With The Pumper in the saddle, an early lead was certain. Longden's forte was getting to the front and staying there, literally raising up the head and neck of a tiring horse, pumping in sync with the rhythm of its stride. Crash believed Princess Margaret would run with a stalking style, sitting in the catbird seat, ready to pounce on the early leaders, when they straightened for home.

The 2:00 p.m. post time rapidly approached. The second race was scheduled a half hour later. Crash stopped by the barn to see if George needed a hand. "No thanks," he replied, "Manuel here, is going to help me."

"You look a little nervous," Crash remarked.

"Just a little stage fright, I guess," George joked, the tension easing a little.

All three of them knew that racing was extremely dangerous. So many things can go wrong from the time Margaret left the barn, entered the paddock, saddled before a crowd, the post parade warm-up, loading into the starting gate, and then the race itself. Every stage carried a risk of injury or acute stress, which could lead to dehydration, irregular heart rhythm, or colic. No one would completely relax until after Margaret was watered off and cooled out, safely back in her stall, munching on hay.

Buying the meal tickets had left Crash with $250 to wager. He headed to the grandstand. At

2:20 p.m. Princess Margaret pranced out onto the track, parading toward the gate in post position order. A mild sea breeze kept her cool, her coat dry. So far, so good, thought Crash. Looking at the totalisator board, he saw her odds were a generous 30-1. If she won, Crash was in for a big score.

He stood in line at the $50 window, hoping no one would recognize him, then follow his action. The two minute warning sounded, as he waited behind someone he thought to be a novice player who could not make up his mind. Others in line were yelling to speed it up. Suddenly, Crash recognized the man from the kitchen.

"Hey mister, hurry up, the guys behind me will want to lynch you, if they get shut out. Bet a saver on Princess Margaret," he said, weakened by guilt at misdirecting him onto the One Horse. Thanking Crash, the man bet both horses: $500 each to win. Crash choked, when he heard the size of the bet, then watched Margaret's odds nosedive before he reached the teller. In a hushed tone, he requested five tickets to win, then hurried outside to watch the race.

"Therrre all in line," announced Harry Henson, when the flagman signaled the horses in the starting gate were ready. "And therrre they go," began the *Voice of Del Mar*. The One Horse, Father's Charm, is quickest away, taking the lead, soon to be joined by The Shoe on Nurse Sharon, with Queen Queen a length-and-one-half further back. Sitting behind that trio is

Princess Margaret, a diminishing three lengths back, still under restraint. Just behind that one is Sugar Stones, and Over Indulge, while the others are content to bring up the rear.

"Around the turn, Father's Charm opens up a two-length lead, hugging the rail into the stretch. Nurse Sharon and Queen Queen continue to duel for the second spot; Sugar Stones is on the move as Alex Maese shifts Princes Margaret a neck to her outside, two lengths in front of Over Indulge. Fathers Charm, the favorite, is beginning to tire, as Longden keeps picking her up and setting her down.

"Sugar Stones has moved up to be second, but Princess Margaret is lodging a bid to overtake the top pair. Now fourth, now third, now second, Princess Margaret circles Father's Charm to draw clear, a convincing winner at 17-1. Sugar Stones hangs on to be second, with Father's Charm a tiring third."

Crash could see George was beside himself, smiling, as he hurried to the winner's circle. Alex Maese was beaming. Paying boxcars, the filly lit up the tote, brighter than a movie marquee.

Guessing his comment to the man in line cost him a grand, Crash vowed never again to break one of racing's cardinal rules. He went immediately to the cashier's window. At a time when a brand new Ford could be bought for $2500, the payout was a huge windfall. He decided to look for a car and bank the rest, minus a small sum for a nutritionist. Weighing only 117 lbs., Crash could not diet enough to lose another five pounds, necessary to begin a career as an apprentice jockey.

Returning to the barn, Crash waited with George, while the groom cooled-out Princess Margaret in the State operated test barn. The horseman's bookkeeper would not release the purse money until the urine and blood test cleared. George never had to worry about a positive; he ran on hay and oats, nothing else. At the time, horses were prohibited from racing on the anti-bleeder medication, Lasix, or the analgesic, Butazolidine.

Crash traded in his Buick for a clean low mileage 1957 Chevrolet red convertible, a ten year old used car destined to become a classic example of Fifties engineering and design. Leaving the La Jolla Chevrolet dealership, Crash was styling. Driving through Torrey Pines with the top down, he felt the ocean spray as he drove the 101 into the town of Del Mar. Always an admirer of swank, George was the first to congratulate him on his purchase.

The nutritionist was not so joyful. When the routine lab results came back, he consulted Crash. He was already borderline malnourished, and his electrolytes were out of balance. Serum creatinine levels indicated he was predisposed to early stage kidney disease. Crash needed to put on ten pounds to regain his health, his dream of becoming a jockey shattered.

"Never mind, Kid," George tried to console him.

"You can still gallop horses at one-twenty-seven. Tell you what, next year I'll turn over all my stable equipment to you: feed tubs, water buckets, saddles, bridles, pitchforks. The works. If I have any horses left, you can train them for me too. I'll only bother you during Del Mar."

"Gee, that's very generous. If you think I can handle the responsibility, I'm willing to take it on," Crash chimed in, aware the only person he could really count on was himself.

Satisfied the Del Mar race meeting had been a productive one, George made plans to ship his stable back to Los Angeles for the Santa Anita meeting, traditionally set to begin on the day after Christmas. The time off between race meetings would be a beneficial respite for the horses. Crash planned to visit Grace, once again.

On Christmas Day, Crash drove down to Frontera. Out of curiosity, he detoured past the Ellsworth Ranch, where over a hundred starving broodmares now stood. Crash could count their ribs. Pastures that were once lush irrigated fields had turned to dust, every blade of grass devoured down to the roots, in a desperate attempt at survival. Several mares found lying in the fields were determined to have literally starved to death.

Following the retirement of Khaled due to fertility problems caused by over breeding, the once mighty thoroughbred operation of the Fifties and Sixties collapsed in financial ruin. The Humane Society was already in the rescue stage. Criminal charges would follow. Ellsworth tried to paint a more favorable picture of himself, blaming others, and claiming he had pensioned aging broodmares rather than send them to killer auctions. The claims were contradicted when a number of the mares were found to be in-foal.

Rex Ellsworth, winner of the Kentucky Derby and a major player in Califonia breeding and racing, was to become as reviled as much as he had been revered. Crash hurried on to Frontera, saddened and shocked into a state of disbelief, despite what he saw.

In the visitor's room, Grace let him know her oldest brother had been shot during an East LA gang war. Crash was certain she was slipping into a state of depression, blaming herself for his death. He wondered if she would ever recover from her incarceration, or for that matter, if she could. He kept the visit brief, assuring her, he would see her again.

CHAPTER TEN

PAROLE

Rather than try to justify her crime, Grace contritely expressed remorse at her first parole hearing. The Parole Board was made up of political appointees, who had no clue about life on the streets of Los Angeles, other than what they had learned from television's Sergeant Joe Friday on *Dragnet*. Grace's life experience defied their imagination. A model prisoner, the Board saw fit to release her back into society. She left with more baggage than she came in with: a four year lesbian relationship, which caused her to forever question her sexual identity, and six years of supervised parole. Crash met her at the release exit.

Grace needed permission to go anywhere outside LA County. She was not allowed to associate with any felons, which now included her surviving two brothers and mother. Additionally, she had to find steady employment or training, housing, see her parole officer once a month, report any changes, and under a watchful eye, when called upon at random, she was required to pee in a cup.

She resented this last requirement, not only for its humiliation, but she had no history of drug use. She had witnessed first hand the havoc drugs wreaked on the lives of family and friends. She never gave herself permission to partake.

Parole wasn't going to be easy, but it would be the last hoop she would have to jump through for the justice system. Not that she wanted one, but as a felon she could not buy a gun. More important to Grace, however, was the lifetime condition that barred her from voting.

"So much for women's suffrage," she told Crash. "Before Frontera, my color closed doors. Now, the felony conviction has shut them tight. We have never talked about the shooting. I want you to know it wasn't for me. I had been violated so many times, I couldn't feel anymore, until I met you. I wasn't going to let that scumbag destroy my precious sister. Now, it looks like I was too late.

"It didn't take long for the boyfriend to drop out of sight, once he learned she was going to have a baby. To her credit, she gave her baby up for adoption to spare her from the same kind of life we had. How is it that guys in the hood can act like such bad asses with their bandanas, a .45 in their waistband, standing on a corner flashing gang signs, yet can't man up and take responsibility for their kid? Tell me," Grace demanded, on the verge of tears.

"It's a shame. All guys aren't like that," Crash responded, "but it must seem so at times. I think it depends on how they were raised."

After a few meetings, her parole officer came to view Grace as much a victim as a perpetrator. He arranged for her enrollment in the recently opened West Los Angeles Community College in Culver City, a town otherwise known for its movie studios. Surprisingly, student aid would come from an unorthodox source familiar to the PO, since his caseload was dotted with some of its more prominent members. The Black Panthers used some of its contributions to fund a program of "...bread, housing , and education...." for African Americans, who by this time were calling themselves Black. Grace's education was secure.

As she exited the drab, grey California State Office of Parole on South Central Avenue, she greeted Crash with the news. "Maybe we could move to Culver City. It's not far from Hollywood Park and only thirty miles from Santa Anita, in Arcadia."

"Yeah, sure. College, you? That's exciting news. Do you know what you want to study?"

"Eventually, I'd like to do social work. You know, try to make a difference."

"Well, I'm behind you one hundred per cent," promised Crash.

Within two days, the couple found a studio not far from campus. Cramped, but affordable. By now, landlords could care less about about color or marital status. It was all about paying the rent on time.

"When Del Mar opens, I'll take take you down and introduce you to my friend, George Brent."

"You mean the old movie star. He used to show up on some daytime black and white movie the TV was playing in the prison rec hall. Is he really that good looking?"

"Yeah, like maybe forty years ago. He is very interesting, though, and always treats me good."

Thinking for a moment, Crash had long ago decided not to reveal George's secret IRA life to Grace. Most people in America only knew of the IRA from the 6 o'clock news, when innocents were killed in a bomb blast. Hell, he thought, she probably doesn't know squat about them. A voice from within countered, 'don't be so sure. After all, she read Victor Hugo. Don't underestimate this woman.'

Looking at Grace, he apologized for the distraction. "We'll go down in July. Maybe drive the ocean route with the top down."

"Crash, you're really good to me. I don't want to pull you down into some abyss."

"Don't worry, you won't. Unless it's into a bed," he chuckled. "You did say bliss?"

"You're pathetic," she replied, smiling.

Reflecting on the stories George had told him, and Grace's own struggles, he commented, "Life sure doesn't go in a straight line, never what you expect, only rarely what you plan, full of twists and turns, and then no matter what, you die anyway."

"Boy, what an uplifting remark. Where did

that come from? Just brightens my day," she said with a hint of sarcasm, smiling.

"Sorry, sometimes I think too much."

"Cheer up. Just don't go all gloomy on me. I had enough of that in Frontera. Speaking of which, my Parole Officer found a lawyer, who is willing to re-open my case *pro bono*."

"What's that?" asked Crash, puzzled.

"Free. The lawyer said his firm does a certain amount of *pro bono* cases, where there has been some injustice and the defendant can't afford counsel. He thinks he can get the court to re-examine my case, since the sexual assaults and incest were not used in my defense, only to mitigate sentencing."

"Good Lord, woman, now you're even talking like a lawyer," Crash ribbed.

"Like I told you when I surprised you with No. 24601, I had a lot of spare time."

"By the way, when will you start school?"

"I was thinking about enrolling for the Fall. I'm praying by then, my lawyer will have some good news. I'll never get hired as a social worker with a felony conviction, so why study for it?"

"Even if you get straight A's?" asked Crash.

"Even with a masters or a doctorate. You see there will be times when I will have to testify. With a felony, I can't."

"I don't get it. Bad guys testify against their accomplices all the time."

"Sure, but the opposing attorney can use my conviction to impeach me. A felony goes to character and calls into question my credibility."

"Tell you what, Grace, if you decide social work isn't for you, think about being a lawyer. You sure do sound like one."

"No thanks. I want to help people, not rob them."

"What about your *pro bono* guy?"

"Look, he's just appeasing his conscience for the times he thought about a case and billed a client for 'preparation,' or the half hour he billed some schmuck for reading a one paragraph letter. There are some who bill out 80 hours a week. No lie," she said, in a tone of contempt.

"I wouldn't know. My old man always told me to avoid them. So far, I've succeeded."

"Trust me, I heard, enough lawyer stories in Frontera. My own lawyer was appointed through the court. He was paid a flat fee plus an hourly rate and expenses. Yet, he didn't use a key part of a viable defense. He milked the system. I got nothing but prison time. It was 'slam bam' without the 'thank you ma'am.'"

"I don't blame you for being a tad bitter. But, it never really helps. You know, with that inner peace stuff."

"You're right. It's hard to let it all go though. Some days I feel I've lost everything, my family, my freedom, my morals. I couldn't take losing you."

Without further comment, Crash hugged her and gave an affectionate kiss to her forehead.

CHAPTER ELEVEN

THE TROUBLES

For a few days, Crash gave a hand helping George set up his stable, grooming the horses, until he could hire somebody. On the racetrack, good help is hard to find.

"I'm going to exercise horses up North, at Bay Meadows, Crash announced. There won't be enough work down here, until three weeks before the meet opens."

"Why don't you just stay here and work for me?" offered George. "I'll pay you more than I would give a groom. Plus, I'll sign for your assistant trainer's license." For Crash, this clinched the deal. The stewards would favor his application for a trainer's license, if he could demonstrate he could handle the added responsibility. "I sure can't do all this work myself," George continued.

"Well, if I'm going to be your assistant, shouldn't I know who you learned from? Not trying to be nosy, but that's how this kinda knowledge is passed along. Not in a classroom," Crash stated, matter of fact. It was true, George needed help. Crash could hear a steady wheeze emanating from his chest, whenever he breathed. "Alright," Crash agreed, "I'll just stay here to groom and gallop."

"Good, you'll learn a different perspective on the ground. And, if you have time to get on a few, I'll pay you extra. Tell you what. I never took you to dinner to celebrate Princess Margaret's win. I'll answer your question then. We'll go to Neves' place, and talk. Before I started riding Alex, I rode Ralph Neves on everything. Then he bought a restaurant, 'The Talk of the Town.' He cut back on riding to concentrate on his new business. Now it has a four star rating, gets top reviews from all the food gurus.

"A few years ago, when he was leading rider, Neves was declared dead after a spill at Santa Anita. The ambulance took him to the infirmary. The valets placed his limp body on a gurney. The jocks' room physician couldn't find a pulse or a heartbeat. The LA County coroner was summoned. Just as he arrived, Neves pulled back the sheet covering him and started to sit up. The mood in the room went from tragedy to comedy. The doctor sent him to Arcadia Methodist and they kept him overnight. He was back working horses the next morning, couldn't remember a thing."

"George, that is a really funny story." Crash didn't have the heart to tell George, everybody on the racetrack mentions that tale whenever Ralph's name comes up. "I bet that doctor about had a heart attack, when Neves sat up. I've

watched him ride, he has guts and talent, everything you need to be a top jock."

After they ordered, George recounted his
training experience, saying he bought his first
horse, a filly, at the Keeneland yearling sale, in
1951. "Her mother, Watermill, won the Acorn.
The filly was by Case Ace, the broodmare sire
of that dazzling two-year-old, Raise a Native.
I turned her over to Red McDaniel and ran
third in a small stake with her when she was
three. At the time, Red was the winningst
trainer in America with a phenomenal two
hundred wins for the year. I hung out at the
barn every chance I got. By then, I was pretty
much retired from pictures. I didn't ask too many
questions, just watched the grooms do their job.
Occasionally, I walked a few hots. Every morning
I was there, I checked my filly's training chart.
A pattern became clear, and I started to gain an
understanding.

"McDaniel ran a claiming stable for the most
part. Some guys hated him, calling him the Red
Raider. Then one day something inside him
came unraveled. Racing had moved to Northern
California and Red bought a new Coupe de Ville
when he got there. After saddling the winners of
both halves of the Daily Double, he drove to the
Golden Gate bridge. He stopped the Cadillac on
the highest part of the span, went over to the rail,
and jumped. No note, had a pocketful of money,
left behind a loving wife, no mistress, didn't owe
the feed man, and as far as we knew he was in

good health, in his early forties. Nobody could figure it out.

"I moved my filly to Reggie Cornell's. He had a little cowboy in him. Unlike Red, he shared a lot 'how to' and 'why this is done' kinda information. A good teacher. His nephew is Ron McAnally, and Ronnie was at the barn all the time. Look how good that guy has done, since going out on his own. Reggie trained a lot of good ones, but the best was Santa Anita Derby winner, Silky Sullivan, the horse his fans called Mr. Heart Attack.

"He came from so far out of it, his backers never thought he would get to the wire in time. Once, he was more than forty lengths behind the field, then in the stretch he just vacuumed them up to win by three. He ran for whoever was aboard. Taniguichi, Ycaza, Shoemaker, they all win on him," spoke George, in the parlance of the racetrack. "When Silky started his big run, they just had to stay tied on."

"Man, Oh man! I wish I could have seen that," said Crash, enthralled by the story.

George, too, enjoyed reminiscing. "By this time," he continued, "I had bought a couple of more horses and retired the filly, I named Waterline, to be bred to Alibhai. Reggie was doing a lot of traveling with Silky, so I moved my horses to Willie Molter's barn. I didn't know it at the time, but I would soon be training them myself. Molter had a string at Santa Anita, and was conditioning the great Round Table. A one-time jockey who couldn't make weight, as a trainer, he won all the major handicaps in America. He was a busy man, very intense and very thorough. He knew every hair on each horse under his shedrow. If one got so much as a pimple, he saw it. He checked to see who ate all their dinner, and who didn't finish breakfast. He adjusted his training schedule accordingly, and never hammered on a horse. He treated fillies like they were visiting divas from the Bolshoi Academy of Ballet. No working a horse all out five-eighths every six days. He won sprints like the Bing Crosby at Del Mar and mile-and-three-quarter marathons such as the San Juan Capistrano, and at every distance in between, turf or dirt, it didn't matter. Then, on top of his game, at age fifty, he had a fatal stroke, the same year he was inducted into the Hall of Fame."

"Wow, that is an impressive tree of knowledge," commented Crash, realizing he could learn more from a man who had already taught him so much.

"Was Silky Sullivan the best you ever saw?"

"Can't really say," answered George. "It's sorta like comparing apples and oranges. Silky was an incredible come-from-behind runner that closed with the rush of a locomotive. The others that impressed me had the speed of a jet plane. They all possessed class and grit. Fleet Nasrullah, Gun Bow, Viking Spirit, and Native Diver rocketed and rattled their opposition into the ground. There was never any competition that could look them in the eye and go by. As good as Viking

Spirit was, he managed to eye ball The Diver in the Palos Verdes, Los Angeles Handicap, and in one of The Diver's three Gold Cup wins. He didn't fold so much, as The Diver dug in, never yielding. In races without The Diver running a hole in the wind, Viking Spirit broke speed limits.

"Then there was the fast and venerable Fleet Nasrullah. There's a reason they called him Fleet. Back in '59 he shot to the front in the Lakes and Flowers and never looked back. I loved to hear Harry Henson's call resonate through the barn area. The next year, Johnny Longden rode him to victory in the San Pasqual Handicap at Santa Anita. With a change in scenery came a change in track announcers. I can still remember Joe Hernandez' rhythmic voice like it was yesterday.

"The dark bay was the supreme frontrunner, going gate to wire for the win. Like most of Nasrullah's offspring, he possessed extreme nervous energy, making him that much harder for Jim Nazworthy to train. If he didn't raise hell in the saddling paddock, he was sure to at the starting gate. But, once Longden turned him loose, he was long gone.

"'Pieman' Johnston owned the colt, and stood him at Old English Rancho, near the Ontario airport. After his first few crops went on a tear, 'Pieman' sold him to a big Kentucky syndicate. A former pie deliveryman, Johnston was shrewd, having the Midas touch whether it came to race horses or apple pies."

"What about Gun Bow? How good was he?" interrupted Crash, not wanting George to overlook any of his selections.

"One of the best," replied George. "As you and your buddies sometimes say, 'he was a runnin' mother fucker.' One day, he'll run right into the Hall of Fame."

"You gonna tell me you never use the F word?" Crash teased.

"Not like you Americans do," George answered, smiling, before returning to the exploits of Gun Bow. "Bred by Maine Chance Farm and owned by the queen of cosmetics, Elizabeth Arden, he was sold for tax reasons at age two, his future believed to be compromised by chronic sore shins. Eddie Neloy took over his training, first giving his shins time to heal. Unlike Buster Millerick's regimen of lightning fast workouts for all his horses, notably The Diver, Neloy didn't like to push the pedal to the metal.

"Gun Bow left the latch like a blazing meteor, then seemed to gear down, while drifting out. Blinkers seemed to help him focus and carry his speed. Not quite satisfied, Neloy began to experiment. Believing the son of Gun Shot out of a War Admiral mare had more to give, Eddie drilled a hole in the back of the full cup blinker restricting the vision of each eye. Now Gun Bow could keep on a straight path, and kick it up a notch when seeing a horse ranging up from behind.

"The Bay's three-year-old season was uneventful, save for a win in the Narragansett

Special. Beginning with the 1963-64 Santa Anita meeting, the newly turned four-year-old, outfitted with the modified full cups, reeled off a string of eight major handicap wins, starting with the San Fernando Stakes.

"This same year, there was a colt back East that scorched the earth he ran on. I never got to see Raise a Native run, but he was all the talk on the backstretch.

"Honestly, the best I've seen may be the winner of this year's Californian Stakes. He's a Florida bred that has brilliant speed. Braulio Baeza came out to ride him. His time for the mile-and-sixteenth may have been one-fifth slower than Fleet Nasrullah's Calfornian, but Dr.Fager just toyed with the field."

"So tell me more about Silky Sullivan," Crash reminded his mentor.

"He won twelve, almost half his starts. When he motored into the stretch, the crowd went nuts. Sometimes he'd just run out of racetrack, finishing second or third. Slop or mud put him at a disadvantage. He couldn't get unglued.

"His win in the Santa Anita Derby earned him a ticket to Louisville, the first Saturday in May. As often happens in Kentucky about that time of year, there was a torrential downpour after the card got underway. Silky's chances were sunk.

"Reggie Cornell was a savvy horseman. Knowing rain was called for, he decided to sharpen Silky's speed in a workout the morning of the Derby, with Bill Shoemaker in the irons. Reggie knew

Silky needed to be up close, if he was to have any chance in the mud. The quick breeze would put him on his toes.

"Unfortunately, Silky left his race on the track, despite The Shoe's best effort to restrain the huge chestnut. Reggie had brought along Silky's regular exercise boy, Pete Kozar. Pete was strong, could hold a runaway train if he had to. Shoe was a skilled jock, but a 103 pound lightweight. Hindsight allowed Reggie to view his decision to use Shoe that morning as the colt's undoing.

"But there are always excuses after the Run for the Roses. After all the hype, fans want to know what happened. Also the owners don't want a loss to negate their colt's future career at stud. In the 1958 Derby, Silky's patented stretchrun was merely a lackluster eighth place finish. Frankly, the long train ride to Louisville, the raceday workout, and the track condition all combined forces to defeat Silky.

"Next he was on to Baltimore for the Preakness, joining the Derby winner Tim Tam in a Pullman designed for horses. Finishing twelfth, Silky was far back of favored Tim Tam, the Calumet runner earning a garland of black-eyed Susans. Silky returned to California, where he was never able to reproduce his earlier form. Gamely, he did manage to win some allowance races and place in stakes, while continuing to captivate race fans with his belated run."

∾ ∾ ∾

George continued to regale Crash with stories about the IRA, suggesting he see the movie *The Informer*, if he ever got a chance. Now and then, George talked of growing up in Roscommon, before he went to New York. Countess Markievicz, a wealthy Brit, was sympathetic to Ireland's cause, founding *Fianna Éirann*, a boy scout organization modeled after Baden-Powell's movement. Unlike its British counterpart, which spurned all things political or military, the Countess equipped her boys with rifles, drilling in formation weekly, and instilled a patriotic commitment to a free Ireland. All the boys joined, including George. Excited by the prospect of marching with real rifles, they anxiously awaited a command to present arms, *taigig airm*. In time, they would transfer their skills and discipline to the Irish Republican Army. They were a force in continuous training, readying for war.

༄ ༄ ༄

Crash fell into a routine of cleaning stalls, brushing horses, and picking feet. Daily, he rubbed down their legs, bandaging them with thick cotton wraps. After the morning feed, he began to cook a mash of whole oats for three hours, to be fed at dinnertime, about 4:00 p.m. He walked each horse for 30 minutes every day, sometimes galloping two or three at the track. Once a month, he would hold horses for the blacksmith. It was seven days a week, before dawn until after dusk. Crash wasn't used to hard labor. He longed to return to life as an exercise rider: start at six, be done by ten.

Like many his age, Crash was angry with American government and society. Lies from Washington about Vietnam casualties were becoming more apparent. As far as Washington was concerned there were two versions of truth, what the public wants to know and what they needed to know. Nothing had changed since the Indian Wars. Sometimes journalists ferreted out fact from fiction, but more often than not, their careers were curtailed as their reward.

Crash could not comprehend the widespread oppression of others, simply because their skin was a different color. He had read enough history to see the similarity in the treatment of nineteenth century Native Americans compared to 1960's African-Americans.

The community of Watts was not unlike a reservation. African-Americans were confined by Sunset Laws or a discriminatory refusal by Whites to sell or rent property to anyone of color. Many properties actually had deeds restricting their transfer to Whites only.

Even those homeowners who professed no prejudice were unwilling to sell to non-whites for fear of angering their neighbors. After all, they may meet in church the Sunday after the sale.

George had opened his eyes. Crash had never heard his parents speak of the Irish in anything but derogatory terms. Despite their Irish heritage, they had become completely Anglicized, two generations removed from their roots. After coming to America, he learned little of Irish history: that it was once ruled by England, there was a revolt, then came a civil war, then eventually a democracy for most of the country, the northern part being ruled by Britain, constantly under attack by terrorists.

The American school curriculum offered less than a paragraph about a nation that gave the world James Joyce and William Yeats, tractors, and submarines. There was never a mention of the 700 hundred years of oppression that took place beforehand. The chance acquaintance with George expanded his world view and the impact of injustice.

For the most part, the American people were disinterested in news about Ireland. Strange, Crash thought, since so many had ancestral roots in that land, and, they all celebrate St. Paddy's Day. George, on the other hand, relished current news from friends and family back home.

A 1940's Philco console radio transmitted global news from the BBC, whenever George positioned the antennae in the right direction. The comparatively low powered signal of Ireland's RTÉ was difficult to pick up. *Raidio Teilifís Éireann*, established a few years after the country's civil war, is the Irish version of NPR, sometimes transmitting in native Gaelic. Crash loved to listen to the old Philco.

George informed him of the violence that was

a daily occurrence, now being referred to as The Troubles. The IRA waged an undeclared war against Northern Ireland's Ulster Volunteer Force. The UVF were bolstered in manpower by the British Army and the Royal Ulster Constabulary.

"Don't be misled by the name, it's a misnomer," advised George. "The RUC is a paramilitary group rather than a police force, whose mission is to protect and serve their citizenry."

Further complicating The Troubles was the divide created by Catholic Unionists and the Protestant population, wishing to remain a part of the United Kingdom. The war soon became a Catholic versus Protestant conflict. Although some thirty years after The Troubles began, there would be a Peace Accord, much animosity would remain.

Catholics and Protestants fenced off whole neighborhoods, separating themselves from each other. Children attended segregated schools, separated by faith, not race. Marriage between the two groups was unthinkable, forbidden by the Catholic Church unless the Protestant future spouse converted to the "true religion." Not very likely, thought Crash.

During The Troubles, car bombings, assassinations, shooting of innocents, vandalism and looting were all a part of daily life. Weapons ranged from military assault rifles to iron bars, clubs, bricks and bottles. Anything that could maim or kill would be served up.

Pubs, water companies and electric substations were targeted by homemade bomb makers, who filled the lethal canisters with shards of glass, nails, bolts and scraps of metal. Catholic and Protestant nerves were frayed by the constant worry for their own and their children's safety. In a single two year period, 500 civilians lost their lives, countless others were injured.

There were peace advocates on both sides, some urging at the very least a scaling back of the violence. Within the IRA, there was a need for continuous recruiting. Most of the rank and file agreed the likelihood of combat, and the tenor of lawlessness combined with issuing arms, was a magnet for unemployed or otherwise disenfranchised young Irishmen.

Innocents were sometimes targeted for the sole purpose of instilling fear in others or to preserve a state of conflict. In one incident, a popular band fell victim to a fatal roadside ambush, its members shot dead by Ulster Volunteer Force militia, symbolized by the dreaded Red Right Hand. With six top hits on the Irish singles chart, the Miami Showband was the most adored band in Ireland. They were apolitical. Having completed a performance in Northern Ireland, they were returning home to Dublin, when they stopped for what they thought was a routine military road checkpoint.

UVF members were dressed as British Army regulars. Nothing seemed out of the ordinary. While searching their Volkswagen minivan, two of the UVF men planted a bomb, which they intended to detonate after the group drove away. This would allow Britain to claim the IRA planned to continue its campaign of hostilities, having used the Miami Showband to transport their bombs. The UVF bomb exploded prematurely, however, before the pair could exit, killing them both, and setting the vehicle ablaze.

The other gunmen started shooting, killing three band members and wounding two others. In the aftermath of the murders, questions immediately arose as to how five British uniforms were obtained. A Luger pistol found at the scene was traced back to a Royal Ulster Constabulary Special Branch agent known as The Jackal. He was not arrested, as to do so would have been tantamount to confirming Britain's connection to the murders.

Among the dead was youthful frontman, Fran O'Toole, who had become a teenage heartthrob. One of his band's biggest hits to top the 1975 charts, *Love Is*, was released posthumously. Stricken band member, Stephen Travers landed in a ditch unnoticed, a fellow musician's corpse covering his body. He later described the attack by the UVF saying, "They opened the gates of hell."

It is a testament to the Miami Showband's popularity that the surviving UVF perpetrators were convicted of murder and attempted murder, ultimately serving more than twenty years of their life sentences. Despite inquiries that have suggested involvement by others, no one else was prosecuted.

Days after the massacre, ten innocent protestant workers were gunned down while exiting their bus, in front of a factory. Retaliatory tactics continued to escalate, increasingly vicious. Vengeance coupled with vigilante justice was the norm.

Public confidence in a fair trial was erased by the institution of the Diplock Courts. England's response to claims the IRA intimidated witnesses and jurors led to their formation, based on the recommendation to Britain's Parliament in 1972, by Lord Diplock.

Thereafter, the jury system was dispensed with for those crimes designated as "scheduled" offenses: murder, possession of explosives or restricted weapons, or the infliction of grave bodily injury; in essence, any act deemed terrorism. These are the very crimes which produce the harshest of sentences, thus warrant the preservation of fundamental rights in any democracy, requiring unequivocal justice for the accused.

In the Diplock Courts, a single judge was the trier of fact. The right to confront witnesses was suspended, although, in most cases, the defendant had 'confessed,' making a trial unnecessary. This was especially true if the accused had been detained at Castlereagh prior to his appearance.

Following the Good Friday Agreement of 1998, the number of Diplock Courts declined, the last conviction coming in 2005. In the thirty-odd years the Diplock Courts meted out justice in Northern Ireland, over 10,000 defendants were tried and sentenced, many of them innocent.

The corruptness of these courts is illustrated by a single handwritten notation on the outside of many prosecution evidence folders discovered since the peace process began: "Not to be Disclosed to the Defense." Like American jurisprudence, the United Kingdom has laws mandating exculpatory evidence be turned over to the defense.

Traditionally, faithful Catholics made the sign of the cross, whenever they passed a church of their denomination. Since childhood they were encouraged to do so, until it became second nature. For those who rode a bus, such an act frequently condemned them to death. When plain clothed members of the Ulster Volunteer Forces, posing as passengers, witnessed such devoutness, the unsuspecting Catholic was marked for death. At the next stop, the UVF would execute each one, administering the Red Right Hand of vengeance before disembarking. The weapon of choice, a .32 caliber Walther PPK, a small handgun, easily concealed.

Coldhearted, callous, calculating men like these executioners could be found everywhere, on both sides of the conflict. Ireland had become a nation of lurking danger.

Some in the IRA preferred peaceful protests by hunger strikes that would garner international attention, if not change. Oftentimes fatal, ten of Ireland's healthiest young men, starved themselves to death in one year alone, the most notable being Bobby Sands. An IRA activist, he became a member of *Sinn Féin*, then was jailed at Castlereagh barracks for the fire bombing of a furniture company.

During the time of his hunger strike, Bobby Sands was visited by representatives of Pope John Paul, members of the European Parliament, and the Commission on Human Rights, in a vain attempt to persuade him to discontinue his fast.

Sands was determined this course of action was necessary until reforms were made. He rightfully believed it would call worldwide attention to the cause. As first predicted by Pádraig Pearse, Bobby Sands' own "blood sacrifice" reawakened a sense of pride and belonging, in the People.

Irish Americans, in turn, contributed generously to the cause, in donations of money and the clandestine shipment of arms. Over one hundred thousand mourners attended Sands' funeral. His death sparked a recruiting surge for the IRA and resulted in added sympathy for the plight of the Irish. In the meantime, unsuccessful political attacks on Britain's intractable Prime Minister, Margaret Thatcher, eventually earned her the title of Iron Lady.

Located in Belfast, the RUC barracks at Castlereagh were a stopping off point for those headed toward an extended term commitment, on their way to Long Kesh. English law as applied in Ireland, allowed for detention up to Seven Days, without an arrest or charges filed. For some, the gates at Castlereagh were a revolving door, set on a seven day timer. Repeated apprehensions without trial were reserved for those whose supposed crime lacked proof, or who would not sign a confession. A block cell, akin to a medieval dungeon, known as the Romper Room, housed the means to produce an admission. A signed confession was a ticket out, permitting a transfer to Long Kesh. The Seven Days were sometimes as much a death sentence as the gallows.

Young vibrant men left there dehumanized and desensitized. Castlereagh could at best be described as inhospitable, a place where inmates were subjected to haranguing interrogations, daily beatings and kicks to all parts of their bodies, with a final swipe aimed at their bowl of gruel, spilling the contents onto the floor, the same floor upon which the warders frequently forced the prisoners to empty their chamber pot.

At the end of the ordeal, the inmate was washed down with a skin irritant, carbolic soap, then scrubbed and scoured with a wire brush. Cruelty overruled hygiene. The inmate would be left to recover, unattended, without medical care. If he was lucky enough to move, he could sop up his meal with a shirt, then wring the contents back into the bowl. It was an invitation to cholera and other E-coli borne illness. Maggots and cockroaches thrived. Literally a rathole, Castlereagh instilled hate.

The facility was named by Britain in honor of

the Chief Secretary for Ireland, who quashed the Irish Rebellion of 1798. Two years later, he was instrumental in the creation and passage of the Union of Ireland Act, which united the Kingdom of Ireland with the Kingdom of Great Britain.

At first Catholics did not oppose the Act, since it provided for Catholic emancipation, allowing them to become members of parliament and thus take part in the lawmaking process. This had all the merit of a pipe dream, however, as King George III voided the provision based on his assertion that it violated his Coronation Oath, specifically that portion which required him to maintain the Protestant Reformed Religion.

Ireland's 'brightest and best' were either making petrol bombs for an unwinnable war, were interned or interred. Universities stood empty. Recidivism was the lowest in Europe. Rather than a source of pride, it was a mark of shame.

Many of those released suffered from tuberculosis, their bodies weakened by disease, and nerves irreparably strained beyond their roots. Prison rendered minds incapable of rational thought. Prior to a prison transfer, inmates rode the "conveyor belt," a series of various tortures systematically inflicted with assembly line precision, a manufacturing process, which produced generations of hate.

Detention and torture at Castlereagh was a subtle, if not clear insult to the IRA, who had fought for generations to separate Ireland from

Great Britain, now bound together by the parliamentarian skills of Lord Castlereagh. Vilified by his opponents and native Irish in general, he later suffered from "brain disease," a term given to syphilis induced dementia, eventually descending into a paranoid state, before slitting his own throat with a pen knife. His notorious legacy was immortalized by the poet, Percy Bysshe Shelley, a proponent of non-violence.

During The Troubles, Northern Ireland fell into a state of anarchy. Social mores succumbed to decadence. Alcoholism was prevalent and divorce was on the rise. Unwed mothers giving birth was commonplace, creating a lasting reminder of the social upheaval. Yielding to the Catholic Church's influence, the law requiring condoms be purchased by prescription had yet to be lifted.

The practice of birth control not only remained against Church law, as it had for centuries, but it was also prohibited by the law of the land. Although virtually impossible to enforce, it served to further divide Catholics and Protestants. Over 3500 men, women, and children were killed in this period, from the late 1960's to late 1990's. More than 50,000 were wounded. Property damage was in the hundreds of millions.

The IRA split with the new Provisional IRA, or Provos, over philosophical differences. The Provos were determined to wage an aggressive campaign of guerrilla war against British Rule in Northern Ireland. None other than Moammar Gadhafi donated weapons and ammunition to the militant Provos. The Official IRA sought a united working class within the Catholic and Protestant communities through non-violent protests.

The battle over a unified Ireland would last over thirty years. The Provos and peace prone Official IRA on one side, battled the loyalist paramilitaries, the Ulster Volunteer Force and the Ulster Defense Association (UDA), who were supported by British security forces and rogue citizen armies.

Both sides were guilty of depredations, but one group, The Shankill Road Butchers, was particularly brutal. UDA made up part of its membership, the gang earning its name by torturing their captives prior to execution.

Those whose lives were spared, were often sent on their way after suffering a punishing "six-pack," the name given to shooting a captive in both knees, shoulders and elbows. The individual would be rendered incapacitated, unable to walk and barely able to crawl to freedom, that is, if he could withstand the pain, without losing consciousness. The few who survived this abhorrent cruelty, were permanently disabled for life.

In 1979, Lord Mountbatten, Admiral of the Fleet, first cousin to Queen Elizabeth and commander of the British Troops in World War II, was assassinated. A remote controlled bomb aboard his diesel powered vessel was detonated. Five pounds of dynamite had been hidden below deck, directly beneath the helm, just aft of the cabin. As expected, Mountbatten stood at the wheel, navigating the trawler out of the harbor, taking friends and family on an outing.

Three others on board were killed in the explosion, as the Shadow V sailed toward the Atlantic, off the coast of Ireland, having just left the fishing village of Mullaghmore, north of Sligo. Local fishermen came to their rescue. The Dowager Lady Brabourne, died the next day of her injuries. Seventy-nine year-old Mountbatten's teenage grandson and a young boat boy were killed instantly. Unfortunately, they were unintended victims.

Seated near the stern, others were critically injured: Mountbatten's daughter, son-in-law, and their young adult son. Still alive, Mountbatten was pulled from the water, his mangled legs almost severed from his torso, causing a fatal loss of blood. Young or old, women or children, no one is spared in war.

That same afternoon, two more booby trap bombs killed 18 soldiers of the British Parachute Regiment, escalating the war. Thomas McMahon, a known bomb maker and member of the Provisional IRA, was convicted of planting the explosives on the Shadow V, although he was seventy miles away at the time the bomb went off. The attack was precision planned.

In addition to McMahon, a four or five man Active Service Unit most likely was involved, yet there was only one arrest. Residue on McMahon's shirtsleeves from nitroglycerine, used to set the charge on the dynamite bomb, helped get a conviction. Such forensic evidence was seldom necessary to convict, once police or the RUC had determined guilt. Sentenced to life in prison, McMahon was released after 18 years under the terms of the Good Friday peace agreement.

−ﭚ ﭚ ﭚ

The next morning, back in Southern California, Grace picked up the *LA Times*, telling Crash there was an article about Lord Mountbatten's assassination, along with "collateral conse-quences." The caption read:

IRA Declares War on Royals
Mountbatten Others Murdered

"Would you like me to read it?" Grace asked.

"Yes," replied Crash, "but remember the British make no distinction between the Official IRA, the IRA and the Provisional IRA or Provos. In their eyes, if they oppose British rule in Ireland, that makes them all IRA," reminded Crash, followed by his opinion on the caption.

"Arguably, since Mountbatten was a political target, he was assassinated, the rest, I'll agree, were murdered. Referred to by politicians as collateral damage, some spin doctor during Vietnam decided it was less shocking and more palatable than to refer to them as human beings."

Grace began reading the piece, "As first reported by the BBC, the IRA has already

admitted carrying out the attack on Lord Mountbatten. A statement from the organization said:
'this is one of the discriminate ways we can bring
attention to the English people the continued
occupation of our country.'"

By killing the Queen's cousin, the Provo IRA
raised the stakes in their campaign of terror.
But, it had the same affect as poking a stick at a
sleeping bull dog. It stalled any hope of a political
solution for a United Ireland, ramping up the
determination of the British to continue ruling
Northern Ireland. The Provo IRA claimed responsibility immediately following Mountbatten's
assassination, a major criminal offense, its
outcome abhorrent to the world.

CHAPTER TWELVE

SANTA ANITA

Waking up early, Crash poured himself a cup of coffee, leaving Grace a note. He was starting a salary job galloping for leading trainer Noble Threewitt, and had to be at the barn before six. Noble was about to let his longtime exercise rider go. "On-the-eye" Roper could work a horse to perfection. If the man said breeze a half in 48 2/5 ths, that's exactly where the watch stopped. Unsuccessful as a jockey, he climbed into a bottle. Over the years, his health declined. Once on a horse, he had balance and remarkable skill. On the ground, though, Roper needed steadying to walk down the shedrow. He was an accident waiting to happen.

"How did it go?" asked Grace, when her friend returned.

"Fine, I guess, I still have the job, but Noble didn't fire Roper. Said he couldn't."

"Did Roper promise to quit drinking?" Grace asked, unfamiliar with the stranglehold grip of John Barleycorn.

"No chance of that. Besides, Noble knows

better. The guy's wife sews racing silks, can't make enough to support the family. Noble's going to keep him on. Pay him to rake the shedrow and clean tack. From all I've heard about Noble, he probably won't cut his wages. The man's got a heart. He says, 'do unto others….' I've heard it before, never seen it much, though. Except in Threewitt's barn.

"He trains for Cecil B. De Mille's daughter, Cecelia Harper. De Mille, himself, had a big studio right here in Culver City. He directed *The Ten Commandments* and *The Greatest Show on Earth* among many others, going back to the silent era. Noble says he's fortunate to be training a barnful of horses for one of the richest women in California. I met her this morning. A class act, who really loves horses. Evidently, she's at the track nearly every day. It has become her life. I think Mrs. Harper would be just as happy working for Noble at the barn.

"Some really good thoroughbreds have come out of Noble's shedrow. A few years ago Threewitt raced Correlation to win the Florida Derby and the Wood Memorial. Then at Santa Anita, he set a new track record with a horse named Page, claimed for $4,000. But, he says horses in Europe are some of the world's finest.

"They come over here for the United Nations Handicap at Atlantic City, and often go home with all the money. Racing is different there. Stabling is off the track. Everyone ships in from training centers, or yards, as they call them.

Like Newmarket.

"Most of the racecourses are grass, some with narrow turns, some wide. The homestretch often has an uphill run to the finish. That last hill weeds out the also-rans from the good ones. Their jockeys sit a little higher, looking to restrain their mounts early. They don't whoop-dee-doo away from the gate like they do here, hustling to the lead, sending all the way.

"Over there, the jocks try to get away in good order, find position, track the leader like a cat; then when they straighten away for home, they set down for the drive. I'd like to go back there someday, if nothing else, just to experience the difference."

"Back there?" Grace looked puzzled.

"Yeah, I was born in England. Thought I mentioned it one time."

"No, and I would never have guessed. You don't have any kind of accent."

"I went to school here. You either lose it quick or the bullies bash it out of you. Same as in the real world. There is always someone or group targeting people, who are different. Hell, the English did it with the Irish for centuries."

"How's that?" Grace asked.

"Well, let me try to explain. In Europe, you had this class structure of nobility, Lords, Earls and What-nots, their only achievement being born into some bullshit line of succession. But, it entitled them to unimaginable power and wealth, which accrued off the backs of the less fortunate, those simply born to ordinary folk. There were only two classes: rich and poor, with the latter subdivided into those who worked like slaves for enough to eat and the rest on the edge of starvation.

"The nobility's power stemmed from their eligibility to make laws in parliament, all coincidentally in their favor. It was all about birthright and entitlement. For those who could afford the fare and survive the journey, America offered hope for a change. But, life in the Colonies wasn't much better than in England. That's why the American revolution was bound to happen.

"The English rulers wanted to hold people down, just like at home. It took one hundred and fifty years, but the people revolted eventually. Centuries passed before the Russians overthrew the Czars in 1917. Before that dynasty fell, it was the French Revolution. More recently, Castro led the Cubans against Batista's corrupt government. They all go eventually. Oppressed people can only take so much."

"That's the way Blacks have felt for years," Grace interjected. "The passage of the Civil Rights Act probably prevented a lot of bloodshed. Things still aren't completely right, but life is better and we have hope. You gotta to have hope."

Returning to the lesson, Crash continued, "Other than a brief time when the commoner, Oliver Cromwell, was in charge, kings and queens ruled England," Crash began. "Change started to take place when Queen Victoria married Germany's Prince Albert. He was a visionary, in the sense he recognized the need for the ruling class to lighten up, to avoid a revolution at home.

"He put into motion laws to lift oppressive practices and open pathways for the poor to climb up the class ladder. The Industrial Revolution helped immensely. It wasn't a revolt against government, but it was a major change in manufacturing and commerce. Competition drove wages and a middle class was born. Hell, those companies weren't going to thrive in the steam age if they hired the sons of Lords and Earls. Most of them didn't butter their own bread.

"But, all those changes weren't going to reach across the sea to Ireland, even though it was under British rule. In their view, the Irish were an uneducated lot, who preferred to speak in an ancient tongue, and were by nature lazy. Worst of all, they were Catholic. They were simply undeserving."

"That whole 'undeserving' bit sums up the way much of how White America looks at Black people," commented Grace. "That's how it was growing up in Watt's. We didn't deserve to live in Inglewood, but we could scrub floors there. We didn't deserve the same protection from the LAPD that people in Brentwood had. The Civil Rights movement came along in the nick of time, otherwise all of Los Angeles was going to explode, not just Watts.

"Even now, almost ten years later, you still

have all that entitlement bullshit going on. The Civil Rights laws are constantly being interpreted by the Supreme Court, because Whites want preference in housing, education, and employment. The NAACP, and groups like them, are constantly taking cases to court to gain fundamental rights granted the disenfranchised, namely people of color."

"You're right," agreed Crash. "That's why things like the Fair Housing Act, school busing, and affirmative action are on the Supreme Court's agenda. True change will come someday, but it may not be until the next century. The Black Panthers and the Symbionese Liberation Army (SLA) don't want to wait that long. They are a threat to the White man's status quo. You watch, the FBI will infiltrate them and bring them down, much the same way as British operatives infiltrated Irish revolutionary groups like the IRA. Its dog eat dog.

"Speaking of eating, you hungry? Let's go out to Bob's Big Boy. At least you'll get served nowadays." They both laughed at how long ago that time at the restaurant seemed. "Promise I won't go on about revolutions or inequality."

"That's alright. Saved me reading a few history books," Grace said, appreciatively, without sarcasm.

Within minutes of being seated, the waitress took their order. *"The times they are a-changin',"* hummed Crash, to the beat of the Bob Dylan classic.

"Tell me a bit about your family. You've heard all about mine," pried Grace.

"Well, I can't top your family dynamics, but I will tell you a little about my great grandfather. He left Ireland with his parents at the time of the Potato Famine. Two older siblings stayed behind with relatives, too weak to make the voyage. How sad and desperate a move was that?" Crash interrupted himself, not seeking an answer.

"A five masted steamship sailed from Dublin to Sydney, Australia, full of Irish looking to escape poverty and starvation. There was always danger on these journeys. Besides storms and rough seas, which could break apart a ship, there was a chance of sinking due to overweight. Greedy captains allowed more passengers on board than the ship was designed for. Some were jammed into cargo holds, alongside manacled transportation prisoners, without any proper ventilation, sanitation, or adequate water.

"Transportation was the punishment for felony crimes, the term of confinement to a penal colony ranging from a few years to life. Once their sentence was complete, they had to provide their own means home. Most remained. Food was never sufficient on these voyages. For a newborn on the journey, death was certain.

"Dysentery was rampant. If any passengers with cholera boarded, it would spread like the plague. Those left behind were tormented by the knowledge they would never see their loved ones again."

"Good God," expressed a horrified Grace, her mind depicting images of the incomprehensible suffering.

"My great grandfather made it though, and grew up to be a self-educated entrepreneur."

"What kind of business was he in?" asked a curious Grace.

"Believe it or not, he raced men."

"What, I never heard of that," interrupted Grace.

"He recruited young men who could run fast, from schools, football clubs, or just see some guy running to catch a tram. If he was speedy, but still missed it, my great grandfather would try to hire him on the spot. It was the old 'one door closes, another one opens,' sort of thing. He paid more than they could earn on a regular job, eight shillings a week, plus meals and housing. There was just one rule. They weren't allowed to gamble. That was great grandad's department.

"They travelled all over. To the Outback, Adelaide, Sydney, Canberra, Brisbane, and Darwin, anywhere it was ripe for action. He concentrated on the smaller townships and tried not to make any repeat visits. On a trip to a city like Sydney, he could get plenty of action in the outlying areas such as Mosman or Coogee. His destinations were limited only by the number of railway stops.

"Great grandad would put forth several runners to race against the Townies' best. Gambling action would be modest at first, while the competition was being sized up. As greed and haste mounted, the stakes got higher. Then a beaten runner from great grandad's team would be put in against a good Townie. Sometimes the odds were ten-to-one or better.

"Then Grandad would instruct the runner to go all out to win, but not crush his opponent. This was the first unveiling of the athlete's true ability. If the winning margin was close enough, Grandad was able to do it all over again, albeit at shorter odds. Might have been the same guy who missed the tram."

"Holy Cow, then what would happen?" Grace asked, amazed that anyone could be so unscrupulous. Despite growing up in Watts, she still retained some of the naïveté of a young girl named Fem-Ahli.

"Depending on how much he pissed off the locals, Great Grandad would either let them win a little back or just head to the nearest train station. He eventually parlayed what he made into a racecourse in Sydney. He named it after Lord Rosebery, which seems seems strange considering Irish history. I read his diary and he wrote a sizable draft to purchase the land. He was three hundred pounds short, and worried how he was going to cover the check before it was presented for payment.

"He probably borrowed the money from some Englishman, who insisted on naming the track Rosebery Racecourse. Then again, he may have bent to political pressure. He needed government permission to operate a racetrack. When he bought the land, Rosebery was Prime Minister of the United Kingdom. Naming it after an English Lord must have made my Irish Catholic great grandad throw up."

"Have you ever thought of going back there to race?"

"No, not an option. During World War II, the armed services took over the racecourse for troop training and barracks. After the war, it was in disrepair, the turf course was ruined, and it was sold for shops and housing. The suburb retained the name, giving permanent glorification to British nobility. Besides that, I couldn't leave you; wouldn't want to. If I go anywhere, it will be to England, when you're off parole."

"I'm good with that," said Grace, pleased she was included in his plans, then adding, "what about your mother's side?"

"Irish too. But, her great grandparents took a boat across the Irish Sea, landing in Liverpool. Educated at a boarding school in Leeds, she met my dad, when both were in the war. She was in the Women's Auxiliary Air Force; he was a squadron leader, flying Lancasters for the Royal Australian Air Force. They met over the air waves, when she was an air traffic controller assigned to his base in York, Linton-on-Ouse. Kind of a storybook beginning, wish I could tell you they lived happily ever after. They didn't.

"It was as if they brought the war home with them. There were a lot of battles. The drinking didn't help. I have often asked myself, who am

I to judge?

"My mother lived under the threat of being blown to smithereens, air raid sirens going off all night long. At war's end, her nerves were fried. My father was responsible for dropping bombs on thousands of innocent civilians in cities like Hamburg and Kassel. No doubt, the drinking quieted the screaming from the maimed and dying he heard inside his head."

CHAPTER TWELVE-A

NEW TRIAL

W hen Crash got home at noon, he was surprised to see Grace smoking a menthol cigarette.

"Didn't know you smoked," he said, curtly.

"Usually, I don't. It's something I started in prison. God, I hate that word. In Frontera, trying to keep from going stir crazy."

"Why are you so stressed right now, things are going pretty good? You're on your way to a degree. Got a free lawyer on board, the Black Panthers in your corner, in case any White guys give you shit, and you've got me. It doesn't get any better than that," he said, smiling, making an effort to lighten things up.

"That's exactly why I'm so nervous. My lawyer called, and the court granted our motion for a new trial based on the inadequate defense of counsel. As it turns out, my trial lawyer petitioned the court to grant fees for an expert to apply that new battered wife syndrome defense to my situation. But, the court declined, based in part on the fact that I was living outside the home at the time and I was not a spouse.

"Nevertheless, my defense attorney didn't raise those issues at sentencing. He just caved in, and struck a plea deal with the prosecutor. Left me to take the recommended sentencing. Luckily, those cops got a hold of the Chief District Attorney, and he told his deputy to follow the low end of the sentencing guidelines."

"So, why are you all shook about that? Sounds like good news to me."

"You don't understand. If I can't clean up my record, I can't get the job I want. And if I can't get a passport because I'm on parole, then I can't leave the country. What if England won't let me in anyway, or if you leave me here."

"That's a lot of 'ifs.' I can see you've given this plenty of thought. Maybe too much. Just relax. Things have a way of working out. One thing at a time. See what the new trial brings first of all. Second of all, I won't be going anywhere if you can't go."

"Promise?"

"Cross my heart."

Several weeks passed before Grace heard from her *pro bono* attorney. He had a meeting set up with the District Attorney's office, next week. He was hoping to resolve the matter without a new trial. He telephoned, asking Grace to attend. "For sure, just let me know the time and place," she answered, excited by the possibility of a new beginning.

At the private meeting, the DA offered to

allow her attorney to withdraw the guilty plea to voluntary manslaughter, plead *nolo contendre* to involuntary manslaughter, a four-year sentence with credit for time served, early termination of parole, and the felony be expunged from her record. Stepping into the hallway, her lawyer relayed the offer. Grace jumped at the chance to get her life back.

Ecstatic when she got home, she could hardly contain her excitement, as she gave Crash the news. "I have to appear before the judge next Friday to sign the change of plea, then I'll stop afterward and give the court order to my PO, myself. He won't get his copy until the next week. Besides, I need to thank him, in person, for all he's done."

"I'm happy for you, and us. I was afraid you were going to take up with the Kools." They both shared a laugh at Grace's anxiety that smokey afternoon. "Listen, George just bought a cottage in Solano Beach. Let's go see him on the weekend. He'll be glad to hear about your plea change."

"He will? I've never met him."

"It doesn't matter, he's heard all about you."

"You didn't tell him I was in prison, did you?"

"Trust me, he's heard worse."

"He'll look at me funny."

"No, he'll think you're beautiful."

Sunday they drove to Solano Beach. The old Chevy was showing some wear, burning some oil and running hot. Crash kept his eye on the gauges, oil pressure and temperature. One needle stayed too low, while the other rose too high.

"We might have to stop in Anaheim to let this cool down," Crash informed Grace, while explaining how the more miles a car has, the more lubrication the parts require because they are worn. She only cared that they could get from point A to point B, not the least bit interested in how it was done.

The oil pressure stayed steady, but the temp hovered around HOT. In response to the 1973 oil crisis, California had lowered the maximum highway speed to 55. That helped the engine keep from overheating, but Crash took it down another 10 mph, resulting in some dirty looks from impatient drivers.

Eventually, they pulled off south of the Disneyland exit, at a Jack-in-the-Box drive-thru, where they filled a jug of water. An hour later they were on their way again, keeping it slow, with their fingers crossed, until they were parked in George's driveway. Steam seeped out from beneath the hood, causing Crash to worry the motor may not have too many miles left.

After he was introduced to Grace, George told Crash the car may not be worth fixing, but collectors were starting to buy them. The condition of the engine would not be of concern, only the body. The Bel Air was in perfect shape, not even a parking lot dent. George's daily driver was a metallic blue Cadillac Eldorado. He kept the

Bentley in the garage.

"Tell you what, Crash. You're my friend. Leave the Chevy here and I'll sell it for you. Drive my Cadillac back, and look for something else. You can use the money from the sale to pick up another car. When you bring mine back, you can take the train home. Simple as 1-2-3."

"You do make that sound pretty easy. I was worried."

"Not worth the stress. In life, a real crisis rarely comes along. An unexpected or unpleasant event, yes. Now the Potato Famine, that was a crisis. So was the Spanish Flu. Come on in, please stay for dinner. I have some T-bones to put on the grill later."

George was born to entertain, regardless of the audience size. Much of the conversation centered on the current racing scene, the re-opening of Agua Caliente after a major fire destroyed the grandstand and the phenomenal triple crown wins of Secretariat, the previous year. George admitted he missed training more than show-business, if only he could defeat Father Time, a much more formidable foe than the Black and Tan.

While Grace was out in the garden admiring George's prized Chrysler roses, Crash updated him on her recent recent court appearance.

"Oh, then this is the same girl the cops came to my barn about."

"Yes, George," Crash confirmed.

"She went to prison, and she and her cellmate

were lovers?" George questioned, unsure of the facts.

"Yes, that's the one. We talked about that. It was a situational thing. She's not into girls. There was no conversion. Man, she's all over me," replied Crash, with a grin.

"It's none of my business, Crash, I just don't want to see you get hurt. You wouldn't be the first guy whose girlfriend or wife left him for another woman. It happened all the time in Hollywood, but the studios hushed it up."

"It's okay, we're cool. Maybe she'll be more than just a girlfriend. I think I'll ask her to marry me. Even with all the Civil Rights Movement accomplished, there's still a lot of intolerance in this country. It didn't just go away with repeal of the Sunset laws. That kind of hate is ingrained in people from the time they are born, reinforced day after day.

"When Grace and I go out, we still get a lot of stares. People frown on mixed race couples. Fortunately, we don't need their approval. I've been looking into going to work at Newmarket, outside London. I still have British citizenship, so working there won't be a problem. My resident alien status lets me work here. Since, I don't plan to be gone forever, maybe immigration will let me re-instate it when I return."

"Funny, the English were so prejudiced against the Irish, but not so much against Blacks. You can't ever figure out bigotry," said George.

After dinner, he handed Crash the keys to his Cadillac. Seated behind the wheel, Crash was impressed by the luxury of the vehicle. Straight ahead was the hood ornament resembling a gunsight. He commented to George that maybe it was for navigation, he had never driven a land yacht before. They both laughed at the enormity of the vehicle. As Crash powered up the electric window ready to leave, George cautioned, "don't pass by too many gas stations, this only gets nine miles per gallon."

"As long as gas is only 54 cents a gallon, I'll be alright," he smiled, waving goodbye.

Heading north on Interstate 5, the couple talked about their visit and George's generosity. Grace asked, "What was he talking about when he mentioned the Spanish Flu?"

"That was the wave of influenza that spread throughout the world with all the ferocity of a tsunami," answered Crash. "It took hold during World War I. The particular strain of influenza had nothing to do with Spain. War censors didn't allow reports of the death toll on their country, fearful of giving their enemies such knowledge. Spain was neutral, so journalists were free to divulge news of the number of dead, making it appear the pandemic began there.

"Following the end of the Great War, returning combatants from the Allies and Central Powers helped spread the highly contagious disease. Some victims had horrific symptoms such as high fever, diarrhea, and coughing blood before contracting pneumonia, only to survive, spiting the Dullahan. Others experienced a mild fever, then appeared to make a rapid recovery, only to expire hours later. Once the disease descended upon a community, its progression was hard to predict. The Dullahan called out names indiscriminately."

Not wanting to hear more about the magnitude of the suffering, Grace sought to change the subject, telling Crash she knew a student who wanted to sell a Datsun station wagon, only a few years old. She would get Crash the details. Both agreed the drive home was less stressful than the trip down, constantly worried about overheating.

By the next week, George called. The Chevy was sold for $1500, more than enough to buy the Datsun. They would return his Eldorado the following Saturday. The visit was intended to be brief, just drop off the Chevy's title and pick up the check. Crash could see George treasured the company, so they remained until the last train was scheduled to leave.

Just a short walk from the cottage, Crash declined a ride to the station in George's pride and joy. Grace, however, let him know she had never seen a Bentley, let alone ridden in one, telling Crash to speak for himself. George obliged, opening the garage door to start the Bentley.

They boarded Amtrak's refurbished passenger coach, pulled by a new French Turboliner locomotive. Seated on the ocean side, they enjoyed the Pacific coastline and the slowly setting sun.

SHERGAR

As the train pressed further north, the tracks diverted inland through the cities of Santa Ana and Fullerton, passing through the seedier parts, where homeless were gathered around cooking fires, drug dealers were selling their wares, and prostitutes, wary of entrapment, cautiously offered their services. Hardly enough to shock Grace, Crash thought it a sad commentary on the American dream. To him, this life style represented the American nightmare.

From LA's Union Station, they took a bus home. Grace made them *quesadillas*, a light meal before bedtime. Once under the covers, Crash could not resist the nakedness beside him. Looking up, he asked, "am I better than Janelle?"

Furious, Grace wedged her knees under his shoulders and pushed him off the bed. Getting up, she screamed, "I don't believe you said that!"

"I'm sorry," he said, ruefully.

"Sorry? You broke a promise," Grace accused her lover. "When I got released, we had a long talk about that whole thing. You agreed to never bring it up again. Now it seems it's been rattling around in that head of yours the last few years. I need a shower. I just feel dirty all over again."

Crash could say nothing, realizing he had opened up old wounds, needing to satisfy his own ego, and allay whatever his insecurity.

"Can I come in and talk to you?" he asked, sheepishly.

"No, just let me be. When I come out, maybe," she replied, angrily.

152

After all the hot water was gone, Grace toweled off. Putting on a yellow terrycloth bathrobe, she sat beside Crash, putting her hand on his.

"You know," she began, "if this relationship is ever going to work, you're going to have to let go of some stuff, and try to be understanding. I come from one of the world's most screwed up families. That should be apparent to anyone who asks me my name.

"Then I go to prison for killing my own father. In spite of what he did, what kind of person kills their dad? I never met anyone in Frontera who did. I told everyone I was in for killing a rapist, an ex-boyfriend who came to visit, and that I pled out because the DA claimed the sex was consensual. I was ashamed to tell the truth, to other inmates. Can you believe it?

"When Janelle started on me, it was like being raped all over again. In prison, money is power, and if you don't have any, sex is next best. Give some up to the guards, male or female. In return, you can get drugs, which you can convert into money. Simple economics. Supply and demand. Oh, and a thing called basic survival in the Animal Kingdom."

"Go on, I'm listening," said Crash, in a contrite tone.

"If I didn't accommodate Janelle, I wouldn't have made it. Who knows who would have picked me out. Yeah, that's what happens to a newcomer, especially young ones. Some of those women have more testosterone running through their veins than an East German female Olympian. At least Janelle was kind, and I could talk to her. We went through all this when I got out, remember? It was the circumstances.

"Don't you think I wanted to run away, whenever I was outside? But, how far would I have got? The whole world was a fence. Frontera is in the middle of nowhere, wearing prison clothes, without a dime. Maybe hitchhike? You think? My luck, I'd have to give some to whoever picked me up. It would be the same as always. And if I got caught, I would be sent to maximum security, where life didn't get easier. Serious hard time. I'd do all eight years plus two or three more for the escape.

"No thanks, I said. I'll just make this work. The library saved my mind. There was no saving my body. It has never belonged to me anyway; at least that's how I've felt ever since I was ten. I thought with you, I could change that."

"Jeeze, Grace, I can be such a jerk."

"Enough of this talk. I need to go to bed."

"Will we ever get naked together again?" pressed a confused Crash.

"Don't look at me with those puppy dog eyes. I need a little time. I've been hurt. But, I'm tough," she smiled, giving Crash a hint of better days ahead.

❧   ❧   ❧

CHAPTER FOURTEEN

THE BLANKET PROTEST

It was now 1976, and Crash wanted to pay George a visit. He had not sounded so good when they talked on the phone last.

"Grace, let's give the Datsun a good blowout. You wanna run down an' see George?"

"Okay by me, just one favor. Stop at an In 'n' Out drive-in for lunch on the way down. I dreamed about that place for a lot of years. There's one in San Juan Capistrano," replied Grace.

"I love that place. Just burgers and fries. I read an ad in the *Student Voice*, when I went to pick you up, the other day. In 'n' Out is adding real milkshakes to their menu. That's for me. One more pound for some horse to carry; but, hey a man's gotta have nourishment."

Exiting from Interstate 5, South, they drove by the two hundred year old Mission San Juan Capistrano. Here, the swallows return every spring. Called the 'Jewel' of the California Missions, founded by Father Junipero Serra, it was built in the same year as the American Revolution.

At the drive-in, a car hop on roller skates brought out their order: two hamburgers, large fries to share, and a vanilla shake each. Crash commented on the aroma. Reaching across for the food tray affixed to the driver's door, Grace impulsively slipped her hand below his belt line.

"Wow! Better not do that here," protested Crash, as Grace began stroking, discretion giving way to desire.

"Alright, but when we get home I'll finish," she promised.

Crash saw this spontaneous exchange as a renewal of their love life, which had been on hiatus, since his comment about Janelle. Grace wasn't one to hold onto an offense, or keep score. Otherwise, she would never have got through prison.

George was visibly weaker than on their last visit, coughing up phlegm continuously, his fingertips and lips a grey blue. Despite his weight loss, his legs appeared swollen.

"Man, shouldn't you be in the hospital?" asked Crash, concerned for his friend's health, unable to ignore George's pallid appearance.

Seated beside a 40 lb. aluminum oxygen canister, George invited them to sit down.

"Probably, but I like my freedom," he said. "The Screen Actor's Guild makes Cedars-Sinai Medical Center available to its members. But then what? Forest Lawn? No Kid, I'm not ready to call SAG just yet. But, it won't be long. I'm tethered to a portable oxygen cylinder anytime

I go out. For now, though, I'll stay right here, until the visiting nurse stops giving sponge baths."

"You won't change. And you are a little stubborn, I see," said Crash, feeling helpless.

"Yeah, you're right. Years ago some friends cautioned me against smoking, that it might cause cancer. Or, just as bad, emphysema, which the doctors tell me I now have. The link wasn't official until the Surgeon General warned of the health risks back in the Sixties. But, anyone with half a brain knew there was a connection. By then, I said to myself, what's the use? You gotta die of something. I just didn't realize I was going to strangle to death, slowly over time. I'd sooner take a bullet."

Talking was an effort, requiring George to purse his lips to aid the air flow. An expanded chest accommodated inflated lungs, giving forth a rattle with each breath. His was a four pack-a-day habit, plus a pipe. Crash could only imagine how badly George's body was ravaged within.

"I don't mean to make excuses, but the studios wanted us to light up. It helped fill gaps in dialogue and was used as a segue to meet some femme fatale, 'care for a cigarette, my dear?'" George said, mocking a common line from back-in-the-day. "A few years ago my wife died of lung cancer. Smoked like a chimney, she did. She was a model when we married. Claimed cigarettes helped her stay skinny. All of eighty pounds when she died.

"The whole smoking thing was portrayed as fashionable, to entice viewers into the addiction. Little did I know, many of my pictures were partially financed by RJ Reynolds, Liggett & Myers and Phillip Morris. On set, we were dead men and women walking, our slow but ever certain demise recorded by a Bell&Howell on an RKO sound stage."

"George, I'm sorry. I never realized," Crash's voice trailed off.

"It's okay. I've had a good life. You know, revolutionary, wanted by MI5, movie star extraordinaire, horse trainer. Married to beautiful women. It's been a good run," he smiled, with a hint of melancholy in his voice. "Grace, did Crash ever talk about me being a wanted man?"

"No, what are you kidding?"

"It's a long story. Ask Crash to fill you in. Hell, Interpol wouldn't recognize me now," he said, as he gagged a chuckle.

They spent the next few hours chatting about the old days at Santa Anita, the betting coup with Princess Margaret, and a wide range of current events such as Patty Hearst's trial and her kidnapping by the SLA, the hostage crisis in Uganda, and the upcoming presidential debates, which placed a peanut farmer on the world's stage. George soon reminded Crash of the unrest in Ireland, the West London bombings and the institution of British Parliamentary direct rule in Northern Ireland.

Headlining this year of The Troubles, was

the Blanket Protest. Previously, imprisoned IRA were given political status, allowing them certain privileges as prisoners of war, including wearing their own civilian clothes, rather than a prison uniform. Many of these men were detained without trial, convicted of nothing.

Effective March, 1976, they were to be classified as criminals, and, like other convicts, they were to wear prison garb. The end of their Special Category status by the British government, undermined the leadership of the IRA over its members, while in confinement. The men refused to wear prison uniforms, even when stripped of their clothes. The inmates chose to wear blankets instead. Unless they wore the standard prison clothes, they were not allowed out in the exercise yard, or to receive visitors.

When they continued to refuse, prison authorities began cutting off other forms of communication: letters, phone calls, and listening to radio or television. The protestors dug in. Other privileges were withdrawn, including the removal of any furnishings from their cell and the ability to empty their chamber pots. This latter restriction gave the term 'smear campaign' new meaning. Soon the blankets were removed, without regard to the temperature.

By this time, some film and photographs were smuggled out, causing an international outcry about the inhumane treatment. With no end in sight, the IRA ordered the sniper executions of prison officers, while they were off duty, going about their daily life. Those living, were afraid to mow their lawn. Nineteen in total were shot over a three year period, before humanitarian calls to end the harsh rules were heeded.

George predicted things would get worse in Ireland before they got better. At times, he seemed like an old war horse, chomping at the bit, awaiting battle. But, in his seventy-seventh year, his body compromised by emphysema, George could barely make it to the bathroom unassisted, leaning over the TV console to help his breathing, before taking a few more steps.

George let them know his old friend, Jimmy Cagney comes to visit whenever he is in Hollywood, away from his New York farm. "He just takes the same train you did and gets a cab to my door. We share some good stories about the old days. My good buddy, Milburn Stone comes by a couple of times a week. He lives over in La Jolla not far from here. You might know him as Doc from *Gunsmoke*. Anyhow, people look in on me. Not to worry."

After promising to return again, the couple began the drive home, not looking forward to LA freeway gridlock. Grace couldn't wait to ask, "What did he mean by revolutionary?" pausing, she then commented, "And did you see him take a drag off that unfiltered Camel, then go for the oxygen?" Not seeking an answer, she added, "That's terrible."

"No, not terrible. More like a shame. Tobacco companies have too much power. George is as much a crime victim as anyone else who smokes. I always thought nicotine was a tobacco by-product. But the companies add it to the cigarettes to increase the strength of the addiction. Once hooked, you're in for a long hard struggle to get off. The tobacco companies rob you of your health.

"As to the revolutionary bit, I have to keep that to myself, for now. When George passes, I'll tell you. I don't think you'll have long to wait."

"No, unfortunately, I think you're right. I feel sorry for him."

"I know him well. Cheer up. He wouldn't want that. Believe him, when he says he's had a good life."

"How about a movie next week? We hardly ever go out," he reminded Grace.

"Wait a week. I have finals. What do you have in mind?"

"*Casey's Shadow*, with Walter Matthau and Alexis Smith. The whole backstretch is talking about it, supposed to be the best horse racing movie ever. Even better than *Wall of Noise*. Several scenes, I heard, are hilarious. Not some corny Walter Brennan, Shirley Temple flick. Based on a true story, it shows the realities of racetrack life, the highs and lows. A down-on-his-luck horse trainer is a single dad raising three boys, one an aspiring jockey.

"He sends his oldest son to an auction with what little money they have saved. Instead of coming back with a yearling racehorse prospect, he comes home with this god-awful looking broodmare, a twenty-year-old rack of bones. The old man has a conniption, until he finds out she is in foal to Sure Hit, Louisiana's leading quarterhorse sire. The foal turns out to be a running machine, winning the country's richest race, the million dollar All American Futurity at Ruidoso, in New Mexico. We should go there someday. It's playing at the Pacific through the month. "

"Someday? Where, to the Pacific theater?"

"No, I mean yes. We can go see the movie right after your exams. I'm talking about going to the All American. Quarterhorse racing is so different. It's like comparing the Indianapolis 500 with the Pomona drag races. The quarterhorse was named for the distance it runs, all out. A quarter-mile, same as a dragster. When we go, we'll see some of that country. It is one of George's favorite places to visit.

"He liked to stay in Santa Fe at the La Fonda Hotel. A lot of movie stars stayed there. Greer Garson loved that part of the land so much, she and her husband bought a ranch 20 miles square, named Forked Lightning. They could have had their own country. Huge, it just needed a flag and an anthem. The guy she married was an oil rich millionaire, who loved racehorses. He owned Ack Ack, Champion and Horse of the Year, trained by Charlie Whittingham, himself a champion and all around good guy.

"George talked often about La Fonda and some of his friends who stayed there, Carole Lombard,

King Kong's Fay Wray, Susan Hayward, Errol Flynn, Clark Gable, David Niven. Can you imagine the hedonistic parties they had? Probably made *Sodom and Gomorrah* look like one of Grimm's Fairy Tales.

"George liked New Mexico so much because a number of Irish Americans had moved there. One even designed the state flag. For them, compared to Ireland, it was Utopia. Even the land looked to be free. Their Catholic faith was not a stigma, as it had been in their homeland. The natural beauty of the place reached out with its magnetic lure of enchantment. Irish immigrants first began coming West, looking for work swinging a sledge hammer, when the railroads started expanding.

"Pickaxe in hand, they also mined silver and gold. Mine operators practically stood in line to hire them. Strong workers, they were just glad to be able to buy food, all too scarce where they came from. Their children went on to become military men, politicians, priests, teachers and a few were outlaws, like Billy the Kid. The native Apaches were not so happy to see the population boom."

"Billy the Kid? Irish?" Grace queried, surprised.

"Yeah," answered Crash. "Both his parents came to New York during the Famine. He later used the name Bonney, but he was a McCarty growing up in Silver City.

"The Confederate Army was involved in a war on two fronts, trying to beat the Union and to conquer the Apache, in an attempt to take possession of

Arizona and New Mexico Territories. Evidently, they failed to heed that historic warning of others since ancient Greece, 'United we stand, divided we fall.' Ulster Loyalists from the Six Counties used it as their slogan, in support of British rule.

"The mountains of Pinos Altos, not far from Silver City, were home to a large number of Apaches, seeking refuge from the heat below and the abundant game shielded by the tall pines.

"Once gold was discovered, every gold and silver miner from both territories headed that way. Thousands descended on the area like swarms of locusts. By 1861, the Apaches had about enough. Greatly outnumbered by the Confederate Army and White settlers, many of whom were Irish, Chiefs Mangas Coloradas and Cochise smoked the warpipe.

"Leading a fighting force of three hundred warriors, they attacked at dawn, securing mines and trapping the men below ground. By noon, they were engaged with townspeople and soldiers in kill or be killed combat. The interlopers were no match for the ferocity of men losing their way of life, raised in a culture of warfare.

"A Confederate Colonel, mounted with his saber drawn, was ripped from his steed, slammed to the ground. Looking up at his adversary, he pleaded for his life. His eyes were met by a red striped mask, the war paint fortelling a vision of victory. Seeing the diagonal black lines on the Apache's cheeks, a vow of vengeance, the officer knew the futility of his plea, no matter how plaintive his cry. Swiftly, a tomahawk delivered him to his Maker.

"The enormity of the casualties that awaited those he was ordered to protect, spurred an officer to requisition an old cannon on display from the porch of Judge Roy Bean's general store. Recovered from The Alamo, nails, snips of tin, and silverware, replaced long lost cannon balls. The shrapnel killed, maimed, and blinded. War clubs, arrows, and stolen Winchesters were rendered ineffective against such a powerful weapon. The Apaches suffered much loss. Cochise and Mangas Coloradas called upon their followers to retreat. Nevertheless, some surviving braves were destined to die unmercifully from wounds infected with gangrene."

"That is horrible. Worse than Watts. Doesn't sound like life was any better back then," said Grace, who could still be shocked by man's inhumanity to man. "So when can we go to New Mexico?" she asked.

"One Day," he answered, not wishing to be specific.

"That will be nice. You're the best," Grace complimented

"Some of the time," Crash smiled.

Chapter Fifteen

AFFIRMED

Triple Crown winner, Affirmed, last year's three-year-old champion, was coming off a win against four-year-olds in the Strub stakes, under Laffit Pincay. He was now seeking to stake his claim as one of the best handicap horses, by defeating his elders in the Santa Anita Handicap, to be run on March 4th, 1979. The Big Cap attracted a stellar field of multiple stakes winners, including Exceller, winner of the Jockey Club Gold Cup over Affirmed, a race in which his jockey's saddle slipped.

"Grace, sweetheart, the race is going to be shown on ABC's Wide World of Sports, with Jim McKay," Crash announced, while she turned some pork chops on the outdoor grill. "Maybe we could watch it with George, instead of going out to the track, with the other 70,000 fans."

"Suits me, but we do have a color TV now," Grace reminded him. "Sure you want to go? Are you worried about George?" she added, intuitively.

"Yeah, I talked to him yesterday. Sounded

terrible. He has a live-in caretaker, and uses a walker if he's not in his wheelchair."

"Not good," added Grace. "I was reading about emphysema in *Your Health* magazine at the school bookstore. Ninety per cent of cases are caused by smoking, which destroys lung tissue. The symptoms don't begin to show for at least twenty-five years. Once discovered, life expectancy is only six or eight years. The article offered some hope if you stop smoking when the disease is first diagnosed. You can improve your lifetime from eight to twelve years. Whoopee. A few extra years of breathing like a guppy. No more Kools for me," she pledged.

"You're right it's fatal. I've got to pass on dinner. Just wrap mine up and I'll reheat it tomorrow. I don't feel too good. Like someone just stole part of me."

"I know the feeling. If you want to go to bed, I'll come tuck you in."

"Nothing more?"

"No, you don't need more."

"You're right, I couldn't anyway. I'm just churning inside."

Big Cap day soon arrived, along with an early spring Santa Ana, blowing a warm current of air. Crash missed his convertible on such days. Threewitt had several horses for him to work that Saturday morning. By noon, the couple was driving south on Interstate 5, not wishing to arrive too early and tire their host.

A young man, in his thirties, answered the

door at George's Solano Beach home. Introducing
himself as Andrew, he had been an orderly in a
Vietnam medical unit. Always generous, George
no doubt paid him well. Expecting the couple, he
showed them to the outside patio, where George
now preferred to spend his days with Duffy, a
black Belgian Shepherd.

On a clear day from there, during the racing
meet, he could hear Del Mar's track announcer.
Unable to attend, for George it was next best. He
still looked forward to the season's opening day,
always on a Wednesday. In his heart, though,
he knew this year's event would come too late.
George extended his hand to welcome his guests,
disregarding their look of shock.

"How are you my friends?" he asked, in his
decades old, clipped British accent, practiced for
Hollywood to cover his Irish brogue. With time,
it became his natural speech.

Still taken aback by his gaunt appearance, they
answered positively. How could they respond
otherwise? George barely weighed a hundred
pounds. This former member of an Active Service
Unit in the IRA's revolutionary war, matinee idol
and leading man, was now a skeletal shell of his
former self. For Crash, it was a heartbreaking
sight.

Talking in halting breaths, between gasps
for oxygen, George spoke of his present situation, "look not even an ashtray in this place,"
he said, trying to laugh. "Thank you both for
coming. I was going to call you, before you

rang. An ambulance is going to take me to the Motion Picture and Television Country House and Hospital, in Woodland Hills, at the end of the month. When I'm too far gone for assisted living in one of the Country House cottages, I'll be admitted to the hospital. Andrew and my son are going to close this place up, then its for sale." Sallow skin and sunken eyes foretold the Dullahan's imminent arrival.

"I didn't know you had a son," remarked Crash.

"Yeah, he comes once in awhile. Got a daughter too. They never cared much for Hollywood. Neither liked horse racing. Probably thought I was wasting their inheritance. When I look at how much I made and lost, they are right. But, I came into this world without anything, and I suppose its the way we all go out. The poor bear death better than the rich. Somehow money seems to give a false sense of entitlement, even to immortality."

"Don't talk, George, give it a rest," suggested Crash.

"No, my friend. I'm headed for a long rest. Eternally," he smiled, resigned to his fate.

The effort at gallows humor fell flat on his guests. Andrew rolled his eyes, overhearing the comment, while bringing iced tea.

Turning to Crash, George spoke, "I asked Andrew to pack up some things for you. I sure won't be needing them. Win pictures, couple of bridles, some Hollywood memorabilia, publicity stills and a few old movie posters. No Oscars.

Rarely went to the awards ceremony. Not even nominated. Rarely, hell! I never attended the awards, not once," a tinge of bitterness in his voice.

"I was hardly in the same league as Clark Gable, but a damn good looking dude, just the same. We turned the pencil thin moustache into high fashion. I made movies like *Racket Busters* and *The Corpse Came C.O.D. Dark Victory* was my favorite. Never auditioned for a movie like *Gone With The Wind*."

"I love you, George," blurted out a tearful Crash.

"Hey, don't cry for me. Like I told you, life's been good. A few weeks on a morphine drip, and I'll just fade away. The last curtain call. Dying's part of life, my boy. Hell, better men than me left the stage, much younger, and in their prime. Look at Pádraig Pearse. God only knows what Michael Collins could have accomplished for Ireland had he lived."

At George's request, Andrew turned on the television to watch the Santa Anita Handicap, just in time to see the horses loaded into the starting gate. Once again piloted by Pincay at the controls, Affirmed broke alertly to lay off pacesetter Painted Wagon, surging to the lead around the far turn. Drawing clear by four lengths to win under a strong hand ride, favored Affirmed's victory marked the fastest running of the Big Cap.

Alluding to Affirmed's previous rider, the teenage Steve Cauthen, George noted, "The 'Kid' has the hands of Van Cliburn, can finesse a horse, whereas Pincay is raw power, at its purest. He can carry one that critical final furlong, if he has to. Of course, they both have been riding about the best horse to look through a bridle, since Man o' War.

"I've seen every Triple Crown winner to come along after Sir Barton. They all belong to an elite group of racehorses, winning at classic distances, scheduled over a six week period, able to navigate slop or run on concrete if the track comes up hard and fast, as Churchill is sometimes prone to do. Hell, track management orders maintenance to tighten the surface down, just so they can set record times. It would be tough to name the best, and, as memory fades, we are inclined to give the nod to recency.

"But, I gotta tell you, this Affirmed is absolutely extraordinary. I always measure a horse by who he beat, and he beat a good one in Alydar. Sham was a nice horse, but no world beater. It was no surprise that Secretariat left him in his wake. Seattle Slew was exceptionally fast, but the one time he bested Affirmed was not enough to garner Horse-of-the-Year. That honor went to the chestnut trained by Laz Barrera, as the voting turf writers took into consideration Affirmed was a three-year-old facing his elders."

"So, do you think he's the best ever?" questioned Crash.

"Difficult to say. We're talking of different eras, track conditions, and distances," replied George.

"Maybe not the best ever, but certainly the best I've seen."

Champion at two and three, and Champion older horse at four, Affirmed followed his Big Cap performance with five wins in a row, including four Grade I victories. At stud, he sired eighty stakes winners, including nine champions, in addition to the victors of the Canadian Triple Crown and Irish One Thousand Guineas.

Obviously tired, Andrew suggested George lay down, to which he agreed. Sleep was almost instantaneous, as Andrew propped his head up, allowing his trachea to clear and prevent aspiration from the pus filled sputum excreting from his lungs. The Boston Strangler delivered a more merciful death.

Leaving the house with the gifts from his friend, Crash asked Grace to open the door to the Datsun. Andrew interrupted to say George wanted him to have a few more items. Opening the garage door, he popped the trunk to the Eldorado, where seven scrapbooks were neatly placed.

"George wants you to have these," Andrew said, in a manner which would deter a refusal.

"But, these should go to his son or daughter," Crash protested.

"Not likely," countered Andrew, "they really have no interest. Besides, George said you are like a son to him."

Crash went to transfer the scrapbooks to the Datsun, stopping when Andrew told him to wait.

There was more. George arranged for the Philco to be delivered to their apartment next week and the Cadillac was to be his. The Belgian would be going with Andrew.

Handing Crash the keys, he said George hadn't driven the Eldorado 50 miles since he loaned it to him. It had less than 20,000 miles total, a far more practical car than the Bentley, destined for a celebrity auction, the proceeds to go to the Motion Picture Pioneers Assistance Fund.

Andrew would hear none of Crash's protests, saying the Philco was as good as on its way. The title transfer was in the glove box and he would find a use for a second car. Grace said she was more comfortable with the compact Datsun.

Driving home alone, in the Eldorado, suited Crash. The visit impacted him to his very core. Sadness overcame the couple before their departure. Absent conversation, the return would give them time to reflect and regain their composure.

In May, Crash made a vain attempt to visit again; this time at the Motion Picture and Television Hospital, twenty miles and a world away from the Hollywood lifestyle George relished. His room had all the accoutrements of hospice care, where end of life comfort is permitted, but no extraordinary measures are to be taken. On prior visits, George seemed alert and reasonably comfortable, while able to stay in an assisted living cottage.

This time he was heavily sedated, now wearing a death mask, facial skin shriveled taut against

the maxilla, a prelude to death. A priest exited
the room, a narrow gold stole around his neck.
Crash recognized the vestment worn for the
sacrament of Extreme Unction. He knew it was
over, and George had all but passed. The venti-
lator and heart monitor continued to whir, soon
to flat line. The Dullahan arrived.

Remembering hearing of an old Scandinavian
tradition, Crash opened a window to facilitate
George's soul departing the dying human form.

For the next few days, Grace could do nothing
to comfort Crash. He was inconsolable.

Both *Variety* and the *Los Angeles Times*
carried obituaries recounting George's movie
career, repeating words of sympathy from former
co-stars and mourning Hollywood's loss of yet
another pioneer from the Talkies era. Bette
Davis, who often appeared as his leading lady,
was quoted as saying what a dear man he was,
finally acknowledging their decades long affair.
Few of the obits mentioned that aspect of his
life for which he was most proud, fighting for a
free Ireland.

No one, at either Los Angeles publication, was
able to confirm George had been a member of the
IRA, let alone a fugitive. George had guarded
his past well. He was not overly worried, nor
neurotic, just rightfully concerned that some
former Black and Tan or Ulster Volunteer Force
gunman would seize the opportunity to fulfill a
duty. After all, these were men who executed
innocent musicians, or Catholics, whose only

offense was to make the sign of the cross.

George's passing was also noted in the *Thoroughbred Record* magazine, mentioning his motion picture career, reporting racing statistics, and winners he bred, including Princess Margaret. Bred to Somethingfabulous, a son of Northern Dancer and Somethingroyal, Princess produced the good stakes winner of the Inglewood Handicap. George was the registered breeder of record with the Jockey Club Stud Book, having arranged the mating of the grey filly to Secretariat's half brother, before selling her with the foal at her side.

৵ ৵ ৵

After transferring to Occidental College, Grace graduated with a Bachelor's Degree in Social Work. She took civil service exams for LA County and neighboring Orange and Ventura counties, and participated in the oral interviews. In almost eighteen months, she had yet to be called. Although the expungement negated the conviction, it was a legal fiction. The facts remained, and her arrest record showed the crime, notating the expungement almost as an afterthought.

She prayed a Human Resources evaluation would be lenient, giving her the opportunity to change her life. Finally, Los Angeles Children's Services sent her a notice she was hired. Two years with LA County would make it easier for her to transfer her skills to a future UK Social Services position.

Gradually, Crash's mood improved as he reconciled his feelings, recognizing how fortunate he was to have been George's friend. He received some promising leads for assistant trainer positions in England. The couple set the Spring of 1981 as their date with another life.

The extra time would give Grace beneficial work experience. Most of Grace's salary went into a savings account in the county employees credit union. Rent and groceries came out of Crash's paycheck.

Chapter Sixteen

WEDDING PLANS

"Grace, you love me, right?" asked Crash, in between brushing his teeth before heading to the track.

"Of course. What a time to ask though, when I'm sitting on the loo."

"No biggie. I've seen you before," said Crash, in a nonchalant tone.

"Well, some privacy is always nice. This isn't Frontera," responded Grace, in mild protest.

"No, and it never will be. Why don't we get married?"

"You're asking me in here? The bathroom? You can't wait until I flush? You're too much," Grace scolded, in jest.

"What, you want me to get down on my knees?"

"No, especially not right now. Just step out. I'll give you my answer in a minute."

Completely disrobed, she threw her arms around Crash, now standing in the kitchen. A thrill of delight in her voice, she almost shouted.

"The answer is **yes**. What prompted this surprise? No one gets proposed to at the 5:00

177

a.m. morning bathroom drill. Dinner and wine, a walk in the woods, a rowboat on a lake, but, not in the john. You are hilarious," she said, smiling, as his hands caressed her nakedness: the small breasts, some extra tummy, and high, rounded buttocks.

"Who cares? Just don't tell our kids."

"Children. You want children?" asked Grace, sounding happier than ever.

"Yeah, to give them the kind of life we never had. Oh, and I definitely don't want a marriage with a 'sell-by' date. My parents went long past that day; Catholic and from a generation that didn't believe in divorce. They were always fighting and arguing over money; my mother bitching about dad's boozing; my dad going out to bars, not coming home until two or three in the morning. Little did they realize, if he gave up drinking, it would solve both problems."

"Alright, Crash, slow down, what's up?" Grace's intuitive senses putting the brakes on her excitement.

"Well, now that you're off parole and no longer a felon, you will be able to get a passport, no problem." Interrupting his reply to kiss her about the neckline and her cleavage, Crash continued, "Then, if I get a job in England, you can come with. Either we get married here or over there. Maybe in Worcestershire, where my parents got hitched."

"Sounds more like a steak sauce than a wedding destination," Grace wisecracked, grinning.

"Wherever you want," she added. "Maybe I can get a job with children's services in England."

"Don't see why not. Let's start looking."

"You never cease to brighten my day."

"That's because I love you," he said, gently kissing her on the lips.

"Are you going to see any of your family, before we go," asked Crash.

"I don't think so. I've written them, but never received a reply. I heard my mom just moves from one bad relationship to another. Crack. My little sister's got two kids. They are already in foster homes. She's being pimped out. The Juvenile Court is in the process of terminating her parental rights so they can be adopted.

"My brothers are incarcerated. Lifers, for breaking the three strikes rule. Doing hard time in San Quentin. The Norteños and Crips are always at war. Their only way out is in a body bag. Everyone is so toxic, Haz Mat couldn't clean them up.

"I hate to give up on them, but one thing I learned in Frontera is that crazy people make sane people crazy. Sane people don't make crazy ones sane. It just doesn't work in reverse. So, I guess the short answer to your question is 'no,'" finished Grace, with an air of sadness.

CHAPTER SEVENTEEN

SHARMEEN

"Och, Da, the bay looks like she's goin' to have her baby." Wearing scruffy barn clothes, with an odor of horse about his person, the twelve-year-old nudged the nightwatchman, asleep on the couch.

Hurrying to the foaling barn, they saw the Aga Khan's Sharmeen circling inside the large broodmare stall, her udder full, a waxlike substance coating the teets, dripping a stream of milk. "Be anytime now, lad," said the father. "Soon as she starts pawing the straw into a pile to lie down on, she'll be ready to foal."

"There she goes, pulling the straw into hill," said the boy, already an experienced hand at foaling. Once down, the father wrapped her tail, then stood aside waiting for her water to break. What seemed like hours, were only minutes, as the water broke and a small head began to emerge.

"This is the tricky part, son. We must be sure it can breathe before the umbilical cord breaks, else it will suffocate. Here it comes. Oh, it's big. Go stroke Sharmeen's head. Comfort her. Keep her quiet. When she has contractions, I'll pull lightly on the baby to help her.

"So far, so good. The placenta hasn't broken at the nose. I'll break it open," he said loudly, trying to control that panicky feeling that goes with the job at hand. "Great, lad, he's out. It's a boy!" His son was thrilled, beaming a big smile.

"Sharmeen will lay there a few minutes until she catches her breath," said, the watchman. "She's bleeding a little, so run up to the house and tell your mum to call Doctor Cosgrove. I'll stay here and put an iodine solution on the naval. He'll come and give the mare something. She's not that bad. Being she's only six, helps. He'll also give her baby a tetanus shot. This one should be standing and nursing by the time you get back."

When the boy returned, he brought along his mother. All three stood back to admire the newborn, beginning to suckle at his dam's side. "What shall we call him?" asked the boy, petting the foal's soft down hair, licked clean by its mother, its short tail swishing back and forth.

"Well, I'm sure the Aga Khan has something in mind," answered his mum. "See those four white ankles, we can call him 'Socks,' for now."

"No," objected the father. "Sounds like a kitten. He's by Great Nephew, all racehorse in his blood. How about 'Blaze,' see that big white one running down his face?"

And soon it was agreed, that spring evening in 1978, Blaze would become the barn name of the first of Sharmeen's twelve lifetime foals. Three would go on to be Group stakes winners, one of which was destined to become the Champion of Champions.

The night watchman was right about the colt's bloodlines. His breeding traced back to Nearco on both sides, another example of Tesio's influence, thereby giving him a license for greatness. A typically awkward foal, never letting his mother out of sight, he could run circles around the babies his age. Six months after birth, he was weaned from his mother. On that traumatic day of separation, he whinnied and neighed so loudly, townspeople could hear his desperate calls. Handled and petted daily, by the watchman's son, Blaze became a people pony, nuzzling anyone who came near.

By next springtime, now a yearling, he was moving with others his age in a large open field, demonstrating his athleticism. He blossomed. As if playing a game, he sometimes let a group of the others outrun him midway across the pasture, then begin a full gallop, charging past, toying with them, as it were. When he took the lead, others would follow.

His precociousness did not escape the watchful eyes of the farm staff who talked him up, whenever they were in Newbridge at Tommy O'Rourke's pub. His large white blaze, four white socks, and his glistening bay coat, together added to his natural presence. The Aga Khan named him Shergar.

The city by the same name, is less than sixty miles from Kabul in Afghanistan, a country which has a centuries long history with the family of The Aga Khan, up through the present day. The Aga Khan Foundation of Afghanistan provides health care and education to the population.

Later that autumn, Shergar would begin preparation for his racing career. Step one was the breaking process, getting him to accept a bit in his mouth and responding to the reins tugging in alternate directions. Saddling the big yearling and mounting him came next, accompanied by a hump in his back and a few bucks, letting the rider know he was no pushover. Soon, however, he became accustomed to the saddle, seeming to enjoy being ridden, whinnying with anticipation, when the groom brought saddle and bridle to the stall door.

After a few weeks of jogging and performing figure eights in the sand ring, Shergar was ready to slow canter on the turf gallops. As his fitness and ability progressed, he transferred over to the training grounds for more advanced horses, where pace and distance would be increased.

There, the Aga Khan gave strict instructions that Shergar was not to be rushed, lest he inhibit his bone growth or developing muscle structure. Lameness has curtailed many a future star's career. By taking his time, the Aga Khan minimized the chances of injury due to the stressors of racing. His Highness recognized in Shergar that special something, the Look of Eagles.

Shergar made his racing debut, near the close of the English racing season. At Newbury Racecourse, in September, 1980, he was a convincing winner of the Kris Plate. The cavalry charge of twenty-three two-year-olds raced up the incline, as they entered the homestretch run. Toward the finish, Shergar kicked it into gear, motoring ahead, much as he had done while teasing his playmates in the yearling fields.

His next start came in the William Hill Futurity at Doncaster. It's not uncommon for debut winners to bounce in their next performance, which is exactly what Shergar did, turning in a mediocre effort to finish second. He came out of the race sound, none the worse for wear. His connections hoped he would benefit from his experience.

Benefit he did, crushing his opponents in his 1981 debut, winning the mile-and-a-quarter Guardian Classic Trial by ten lengths, at Sandown. Among the seventy thousand spectators on hand were Crash and Grace, having made the trip from Heathrow airport, just in time to glimpse the next European Horse of the Year. Top hats and fascinators all but obliterated their view. Neither were disappointed, determined to arrive earlier next time.

Returning to their rented Mini-Minor, excited about their first day in England, the couple drove to Newmarket, where Crash was to begin a job as assistant trainer. Crash was not prepared for the novelty of driving on the opposite side to America. At first the gearshift seemed wrongly placed, left of the steering column. When not thinking, he kept getting in the passenger side to drive. Soon he would adjust, he knew.

But as to the time it took to travel any distance, that he believed, would take a bit of getting used to. He had learned to drive where 65 to 70mph was the norm. It was well over a two hour drive for the hundred miles to Newmarket. Upon arrival they got dinner in a local public house; prawns, pork pies and apple tarts, with a pint.

There was a vacancy at Meadow House, close to the training center, which would suit the couple until they got their bearings, finding someplace long term. Tomorrow morning, Crash would start work.

Grace had a meeting with Suffolk County Social Services, her mailed application approved for hire, pending an in person interview. As she had done for LA County, she would have to explain the circumstances of her conviction. Things were coming together for the pair, thanks to some pre-planning and good timing.

That first week was a busy one for both of them. Fundamentally, the jobs were the same as in the States, but there were differences in procedure. Grace had to clear all decisions on casework with a supervisor, Crash on the other hand was given plenty of latitude with the caveat he produce results. His charges had to be racing fit by the opening of Ascot in mid-June.

In America, thoroughbreds are trained for speed, the predominant distance being six furlongs on the dirt. Horses there are usually galloped or cantered on the racetrack a mile in about 2 ½ to 3 minutes, four days a week, then given a full-run speed workout at four or five furlongs on the fifth day, an unintentioned recipe for lameness. Crash quickly learned this regimen would produce a runner that exploded from the starting gate to lead the field by daylight, only to fade around the turn and tire badly in the uphill stretch run.

Observing such greats as Henry Cecil, trainer of multiple champions and Michael Stoute, trainer of Shergar, prompted Crash to convert his program to the European style of conditioning. Sometimes, horse and rider went out for more than an hour, long walks and cantering three to four miles, on undulating turf gallops, designed to prepare the racehorse for the challenging configuration of the European courses. By the end of May, horses he conditioned were returning to the stables, bright-eyed and ready for more. A few extended workouts were scheduled, so as to have them set for Ascot.

Meanwhile, Grace was learning the only difference between child abuse and neglect in Suffolk County and the dysfunction she witnessed in Los Angeles was the postal code.

The couple decided to move into a flat on Cheveley Road, in the township of Newmarket. Smaller than the studio in Culver City, yet much pricier, they would be making up the difference saving on petrol. With gasoline prices pushing ninety cents a gallon, before leaving the U.S., they were shocked to find the cost tripled when they filled up the Mini-Minor. Whenever they could, they would travel by bus or train. Returning the Mini to Europcar rental agency in nearby Cambridge, they were relieved it took only six more litres.

Looking to step up in size and comfort, the couple bought a used late 70's Humber Sceptre, still capable of 20 mpg. After driving George's Eldorado, Crash complained the Mini felt like he was riding on a skateboard, he was so low to the ground. Deciding to take the Humber on a leisurely Sunday drive, they headed toward Buckingham Palace, which had been first on their wish list of places to visit when they were planning their adventure to the UK.

Upon returning home to their new flat, the couple decided to make an appointment for a civil marriage at the Register Office, having already given the requisite seven day notice of their intent to marry.

When the big day arrived, Grace wore a strap-less light pink tafetta, with a matching veiled pillbox. Not wishing to appear taller than she already was, she wore inexpensive matching pink satin ankle strap flats. Crash rented a simple dark blue tuxedo, his first; since galloping at Rex Ellsworth's ranch had taken the place of his senior prom.

The rain and wind negated any thoughts Crash might have of walking the short distance to the Registry, much to Grace's relief. Following a mutual 'I do,' a plain platinum wedding band cemented their betrothal, a testament to their opposition to "blood diamonds."

Although busy preparing a string of young inexperienced two-year-olds, Crash paused as often as he could to observe Shergar go through his daily regimen. Despite Shergar's loss at the end of his two-year-old year, Crash remained certain Shergar was a super star in the making. As far as Crash was concerned, Shergar could outrun the wind.

A cooling nighttime rain preceded the morning's foggy mist, hiding the future champion from view. Crash noticed Michael Stoute at the rail, stopwatch in hand, peering through the heavy dew, trying to pick out his horses. Some fellow trainers teased him that he wouldn't be able to time this morning's trial. Good naturedly, Michael responded with an old racetrack axiom, "time only matters if you're trying to catch a train."

Moments later, Crash glimpsed the white blaze of Shergar bursting through the cloud, pulling decisively clear of his workmate. It was during early morning training that Crash most often missed his friend George, painfully so.

Horse and rider eased up past the finish, trotting back to Michael to be debriefed. Still some years away from being knighted, Michael hired only the best, and would get a clear picture of how Shergar performed, notwithstanding his obscured view.

Shergar's next start came in the Group III

Chester Vase, run on the left-handed one-mile course at Chester Racetrack. The configuration was virtually a continuous turn, requiring a horse to run on his left lead almost the entire mile-and-one-half distance, making his effort all that more tiresome.

Unlike a straightaway, acceleration is made difficult by the inability to switch leads. Nevertheless, Shergar's twelve length margin of victory surpassed his ten length win in the Guardian Stakes, stamping him as the early favorite for the Epsom Darby. Although spelled the same as Kentucky's derby, Crash could never comprehend how his fellow countrymen pronounced derby as if spelled *ar*.

Nicknamed the Choirboy, the cherubic faced nineteen-year-old Walter Swinburn, Shergar's regular jockey, had a three week suspension for careless riding looming on the horizon. His extensions almost exhausted, he would be fortunate to ride the Darby in June. Regardless, the newlyweds planned to be there, wearing the customary fine attire mandated of attendees.

Over the ensuing weeks leading up to the Darby, Crash watched the magnificent Shergar train nearly every morning. Not that America hasn't had its share of outstanding racehorses, he thought, especially Secretariat, Seattle Slew, and Affirmed, winners of the triple crown during the 70's. But, to the horseman in Crash, Shergar displayed a presence, a fluidity of motion, and raw untapped talent not likely to be seen again.

∾ ∾ ∾

CHAPTER EIGHTEEN

EPSOM DARBY

For the highpoint of the British racing season, all manner of royalty are usually present. The 1981 edition was no exception, attended by Queen Elizabeth and Prince Phillip, accompanied by their son Prince Charles and his fiancée, Diana Spencer, who he would marry the following month. Everyone there dressed in their best. Like most racetracks throughout England, Epsom has a dress code for various ticketed enclosures. The most expensive areas require men to wear black or grey morning coats, top hats and ties. Women wear a hat and formal dress. Fascinators of every imaginable design are the preferred headwear of the ladies. Shorts or pants are prohibited. An exception to the dress code is the infield, which more often than not, resembles Woodstock.

Security was extremely tight. Crash tried to finagle passes to the stabling area to no avail. He settled on a comparatively modest priced ticket to the grandstand section, which required coat and tie, fancy dress and hat. The crowd was such, that had he waited until race day to get tickets, they would have been shut out. Early on the third of June, Mr. and Mrs. set out by train to Tattenham Corner Station.

On the way, Crash, by now a walking history book, described the significance of Tattenham. "Not only is it a sharp bend requiring a horse to be on his left lead, it is also the beginning of an uphill run to the finish line. Emily Davison, like America's Susan B. Anthony, was an activist for women's right to vote. At the 1913 Darby, she threw herself in front of Anmer, the entry owned by King George V."

"Oh, my God, how horrible!" exclaimed Grace. "She must have been desperate to be heard. I can relate to her frustration. A lot of women in Frontera can too."

"Tattenham Corner gave her the perfect opportunity, because the field needed to slow as they made the turn, enabling her to pick out the King's horse. Unconscious after being trampled, she died a few days later, becoming a martyr of the voting rights movement, whose slogan was 'Deeds Not Words.' To some extent her death was in vain, as it was fifteen more years before Parliament finally gave women the vote."

Later that Wednesday, in the Jockeys' Room, the Choirboy dressed in His Highness the Aga Khan's distinctive Irish green silks, with red epaulettes. Stepping onto the the oversized Toledo scales with saddle and weights, the needle stopped at 126 lbs., the prescribed amount each three-year-old carried. The jockey's valet pulled a matching green cap cover over his safety helmet, exempted from the weigh-in.

The horses entered their assigned saddling stalls, where trainers waited to perform the final task, before sending them out for the most prestigious race of their careers. The jockeys entered the paddock single file, as the horses were led into the ring. Each rider met with the owner and trainer to discuss race strategy. Some were greeted with a simple, 'Ride him like you own him.' Based on how the race was expected to unfold, others received complex instructions, none of which they could ever remember, and none of which ever materialize as predicted.

The handlers led the horses onto the track for the post parade in numbered order. Shergar wore saddle cloth number 18, signifying he would break from the gate farthest from the inside rail. Some horses were restless, while waiting for the others to load. There was a hush over the crowd of 100,000. Crash and Grace were on their tiptoes, unfortunately so was everyone else. Grace removed her fascinator, allowing those behind her a better view. The announcer called, "two back," pausing momentarily, while an assistant starter walked Shergar into the starting gate.

The commentator announced: "And they're away in good order for the Epsom Darby, Shergar tardy from the gate, as the horses make their way down the short straight. Riboretto and

Scintillating Air are going for the lead. Glint of Gold is shuffled back as Shergar is moving up, three lengths from the front as the field travels around the bend on the left handed course. At the run up the hill, Silver Seas moves into contention, just ahead of Robellino a length and one-half to the good of Waverly Hall, having now cleared the back marker.

Riboretto edging clear, soon to be joined by Silver Seas, as the field exits the backstetch run, rounding Tattenham Corner, four furlongs from home. The top pair are head-to-head for the lead, with Shergar ranging up on their outside. Waverly Hall is dropping back, as the field begins the final uphill run.

Glint of Gold is running fourth, five lengths behind the top trio. Scintillating Air moves quickly toward the rail, inside Glint of Gold, ready to claim a share. Jockey Swinburn taps Shergar on the shoulder, letting him know it's time to leave. It must be time, Shergar is hanging his tongue out, his customary sign of a peak performance. With an electrifying turn of foot, Shergar begins to draw clear.

Two furlongs from home, Shergar is widening his margin by three, by four, now by five, just cruising toward victory. Glint of Gold overtakes Silver Seas with Riboretto dropping back, as Scintillating Air goes between horses, to be third. But, it's Shergar they'll have to catch, as the odds on favorite extends his margin by ten lengths, geared down, simply dominating this Darby field."

Shergar had won by the proverbial "length of the stretch" over the grueling distance of 1½ miles, defeating the best three-year-olds that could be assembled.

Before the outbreak of the Great War, the racegoing public witnessed the blazing speed of The Tetrarch, a spotted grey wonder, never beaten. Then came the 1936 Darby record setting Mahmoud, a grey descendant of The Tetrarch, by now an established influence. Together, they teamed to form the best of the century, sometimes a tentative title generally bestowed by the eyes of the beholder, but still not granted lightly. *Timeform* declared The Tetrarch to be the best two-year-old in the world, eventually proclaiming him best of the twentieth century.

After his win, *The Daily Mirror* and *Guardian* hailed Shergar as the best of the century, clearly a superhorse, a supposition Crash became certain of watching that foggy morning workout at Newmarket.

Waiting at the train station, Crash confided to Grace he had never seen or heard of a performance such as Shergar's. They started making plans to see his next race, the Irish Derby, three weeks away. The ferry ran daily from Holyhead across the Irish Sea to Dublin. From there, it is a one hour bus ride to the Curragh. Crash couldn't wait.

The two-year-olds assigned to Crash were progressing in line with their level of maturity. Depending on the sire and dam, some showed precocity and a readiness to run. Others just couldn't get it together, unsure of what was expected of them. Frightened of the starting gate, they were oftentimes reluctant to load or break, once in, they were dangerously restless.

Some refused to go to the front, preferring the comfort of the herd. Others were unwilling to change over to the correct lead, without prompting from the rider. Most of these 'learning disabilities' would disappear in time, usually by their three-year-old season. A good horseman, like a good teacher, doesn't push their pupil beyond limits.

CHAPTER NINETEEN

IRISH DERBY

A festive mood was evident aboard the two tone green on green double decker, taking a direct route to The Curragh. Built in Ireland, with right hand drive, comfort may have been forsaken for economy, but from their seat on the top deck, Crash and Grace were afforded a panorama of lush countryside. Stud farms abounded, rivaling those of Kentucky.

Passing the Irish National Stud, a seatmate informed them this was home to Ahonoora, another descendant of The Tetrarch, whose progeny were highly sought after at the major sales, notably Tattersalls and Goffs. Eventually siring nine champions, Ahonoora shows up in the pedigree of Kentucky Derby and Dubai World Cup winner, Animal Kingdom, himself now retired to stud. Ahonoora is also the brood-mare sire of America's Horse-of-the-Year, and three-time Champion Older Mare, Azeri.

The legacy of The Tetrarch is assured through Epsom Darby winner Golden Horn, victor in the 2015 prestigious Prix de l'Arc de Triomphe at Longchamp, sired by champion Cape Cross, whose damsire is none other than Ahonoora.

The crowd at The Curragh was every bit as large as the one at Epsom. The dress code was fashionably upscale, sans the pretentious top hats and morning coats of the English Darby. Crash wore a Donegal tweed blazer, while Grace looked stunning in a blue chiffon, trimmed in pink. A wide brimmed fascinator, slightly tilted, completed her outfit. From their spot at the furlong marker, they would have a good look at the field rounding the turn for home before making the final uphill run. Excitement ran through the crowd like electric current.

As the horses entered the final, right-handed bend, Kirtling held a strong advantage, but could do no more when roused, with Shergar looming to his outside, and Cut Above along the rail. Champion jockey, Lester Piggott replacing the suspended Choirboy, never uncocked his stick. Instead, he clucked to his mount, looking back over his shoulder, drawing clear by seven, while winning "in an exercise canter." The voltage amped up as the crowd went wild, having witnessed a racing rarity: the completion of the English and Irish Derby Double.

Overjoyed at seeing racing history, the couple began planning to see Shergar's next race scheduled in July, the Group One, King George VI and Queen Elizabeth Stakes. Shergar was to be re-united with The Choirboy to compete in yet another race at one-and-one-half miles; this time against the best older horses in the UK and Europe.

Ascot's right-handed course, maintained to perfection, would offer Shergar a chance to join the elite few, which succeeded in taking home the Derby Double and the King George, particularly the incomparable Nijinsky, and Grundy, another son of Great Nephew.

Crash explained it is always a daunting assignment for a three-year-old to win against older horses, especially in July, when chronologically they are significantly closer to age three than four. There is a difference in both physical and mental maturity. The four-year-old gelding, Onion, defeated the great Secretariat following his triple crown victories. Crash stated that difference was the only thing to get Shergar beat. For the first time he was meeting battle hardened veteran stake horses.

Crash continued to describe the entrants. Master Willie was coming off wins in the Coronation Cup and Eclipse Stake; Light Cavalry, a speedy front-runner, had won the previous year's edition of the St. Leger. They were joined by Fingal's Cave, victor in the Cumberland Lodge Stakes at the same distance, over this same course, an advantage not to be overlooked by longshot punters. The handicapping lesson was interrupted by the call.

"Racing up the back straight, past the half-mile marker, Light Cavalry is just in front of Master Willie, the top pair two lengths ahead of the others as the field enters the turn, three-quarters

of a mile from home. Master Willie has taken the
lead by a length-and-one-half over Light Cavalry,
now beginning to retreat.

"French Oaks victress Madame Gay looms into
contention, pulling away from Fingal's Cave,
leaving Shergar boxed in on the rail. Now getting
clear, Shergar launches a strong bid, full of run,
putting away Fingal's Cave in a few strides,
charging up Madame Gay's inside, to draw away
'in tremendous style!' Madame Gay hangs on to
be a resolute second, two lengths ahead of the
hard trying Fingal's Cave, finishing third."

"Wow! Did you see that? Shergar is awesome!
A World Beater!" shouted a jubilant Crash, to
no one in particular, just to everyone at Ascot.
Driving the Humber back to Cheveley Road, he
couldn't stop talking. "More impressive than
Secretariat, better than Native Diver," he went
on, not realizing he was comparing apples to
oranges. Both earned American championship
honors on the dirt, running at a shorter distance.
But, Crash didn't care. He had just witnessed
the second coming of Pegasus.

The next day he visited Shergar at Michael
Stoute's training yard in Newmarket. Not that
visitors were welcomed, but Crash couldn't
resist. Since he was now a part of the local racing
scene, he was allowed a brief hello. Shergar was
stretched out taking a mid-morning nap, after
cleaning up a breakfast of crimped oats.

Several opened bales of straw were spread
evenly throughout the stall, banked against the

walls to protect him in case he rolls over. If satin sheets were practical, he would of been tucked in. The glint in his eye and shine to his coat, confirmed the race took little to nothing out of him.

Next on Shergar's calendar was the St. Leger, run on the left-handed Doncaster course, in September. Crash and Grace debated whether they should go, a three hour, 200 mile train ride each way. "How could they not?" they decided.

Crash expressed concern that at some point in a race, lactic acid kicks in. Muscle fatigue causes a racehorse to tire and flatten out. Previous hard races, time between starts, weight, distance, and genetic make-up play a role.

Shergar had run four times in two months, weighted at 126 lbs. With all four races at one-mile-and-four furlongs, he was now going to be asked to go a mile-and-seven furlongs. He would be meeting other good three-year-olds like Cut Above and Glint of Gold. Although he had defeated this pair before, they had skipped a few races in between. Shergar, on the other hand, danced all the dances.

The couple boarded the train at the Cambridge station, catching a six a.m. Doncaster Special. A shuttle service enabled them to complete the last leg of the trip. Once inside the enclosure, they found their seats high up in the grand-stand, which would afford them a good view of the entire pear shaped turf course.

After a buffet breakfast of eggs, bacon and scones, they settled in, conversing with nearby

fans about Shergar's history making achieve-
ments. Crash stated the added distance might
be his undoing, saying he was not about to
bet on him at odds-on. The others responded
by claiming Shergar was unbeatable. Out of a
sense of loyalty, Crash refrained from wagering
against him, certain he would jinx Shergar's
chances if he did so.

Breaking from gate 7, on the far outside of
a seven horse field, Shergar was away slowly,
content to lag in mid-pack. Up a short hill, then
sweeping left around the bend, Shergar moved
into contention a length-and-one-half behind
Kirtling and Glint of Gold. That flashy chestnut
started drawing on even terms with Cut Above,
as Bustomi and Lester Piggott took over the lead.
Around the final turn, Bustomi was struggling to
hang on, Glint of Gold rushed up on his outside,
with Shergar looming the main danger.

Three furlongs from home, Shergar poked his
head in front, then began to fade. Cut Above
stayed along the rail behind the top flight, while
Glint of Gold went to the front, with Shergar still
a close third. The top four sprinted for the wire,
but Shergar failed to sustain a rally. Quickly, Cut
Above saw daylight, surging between Shergar and
Glint of Gold, holding sway to the wire. For the
first time, Shergar could not keep up, finishing a
far back fourth behind Bustomi, and second place
finisher Glint of Gold, a horse Shergar annihilated
at Epsom. Likewise Shergar soundly defeated the
winner, Cut Above, when they met at the Curragh.

Instead of loud cheering from those who backed Cut Above, you could hear a pin drop. The silence was deafening. A nation's hero had fallen. Crash was not surprised, given his own pre-race assessment. Speaking in the parlance of a true racetracker, Crash declared to those nearby, "Shergar ran his eyeballs out. Might have win it at a mile-and-a-half. After all, he had the lead three furlongs from home." Crash was convinced the added distance beat Shergar.

With a little time to spare before they boarded the return train to Cambridge, the couple took a dinner-to-go back to the station. The Old Angel Pub packaged Scotch eggs, cooked with sausage meat, coated in bread crumbs, then fried. Into the box went two slices of pork pie and custard tarts for dessert. "Nothing like good food when you've had a disappointment," extolled Crash, with a raised eyebrow, taking Grace's arm as they crossed the street.

CHAPTER TWENTY

ERINS ISLE

"Word around Newmarket today is the Aga Khan plans to retire Shergar to the breeding shed," Crash announced, when Grace got in from work. "There is really only one more race for him, and that's the Prix de l'Arc de Triomphe, at Longchamp, in Paris. But, it's run at a mile-and-a-half against older horses, the best in Europe. After yesterday's poor showing, it only makes sense to stop on him. He doesn't have anything left to prove, so there is no reason to run him next year."

"Hmmmn," murmured Grace. "With Shergar gone, do you suppose we could go back to America. It's hard to believe, but I miss LA. Don't get me wrong, I like it here, but things are different. Dinner last night is a good example."

"Really?" Crash asked, looking for verification.

"Yes, I would like to. I called my old supervisor, and with a little paper work I can get my old job back," Grace answered, affirmatively.

"Apparently, you have given this some thought," Crash winked, not wishing his remark to be interpreted as sarcastic.

"Well, truth be known," he continued, "I prefer *huevos rancheros* to Scottish eggs. I'll put the Humber up for sale, and we'll give our notice here at the flat and work. We can leave in about thirty days." He had barely got out the words, when Grace jumped into his arms, plunging her tongue to meet his.

"You know I just love your 'jump-up' kisses," he laughed.

The day before they were to fly out of Heathrow, they took the train to London, deciding they couldn't leave without seeing some of the sights. Taking a short bus tour, they saw St. Paul's Cathedral, Piccadilly, and Tower Bridge.

Afterward, they hopped another bus to Stonehenge and Oxford. Crash soaked up the history. Grace, not so much. At day's end, they shopped and dined at Harrods, before spending the night at Shepiston Lodge, close to the airport.

LAX was as chaotic and crowded as when they left. Stepping out of Baggage Claim to hail a cab, they were immediately hit by eye-stinging smog, a partial reminder of why they went to Newmarket. After a night's rest at a Motel 6, with a weekly rate, they began the chore of finding a place to live.

Grace had an interview in two days, while Crash could begin freelance exercise work the next day. Not wanting to part with the car given to him by George, he had put the Eldorado in one of the many storage facilities springing up all over LA. By Thanksgiving, they hoped to be settled. Their former landlord had an upcoming vacancy, which suited the couple.

Crash bought a boxy used Volvo for Grace, saying it was time to put safety ahead of style. Only 'find employment' remained on the to do list, and that was mere days away from being crossed off.

Predictably, Crash was able to get on ten or more horses each morning, at eight dollars a head. He missed his position at Newmarket, but liked the year round racing calendar that Southern California's mild weather makes possible. He became a regular at Charlie Whittingham's barn, one of a handful of gallop boy's capable of restraining a tough horse. Ellsworth had taught him well.

But, of all the exercise riders on the grounds, none was as good a hand as the veteran, Tuffy Morlan. A 118 lb. lightweight, he came by his moniker legitimately, able to anchor lightning. He had been the regular exercise boy for Your Host in the 1950's, sometimes using a hammer-lock to keep the powerful grey colt from running off. The winner of the 1949 Del Mar Futurity, he conquered a good Santa Anita Derby field the following year. Born with crooked neck, the almost white stallion went on to become a major handicap star.

Bred by Tinsletown movie mogul, Louis B. Mayer, head of MGM, the colt was heavily insured. Along the backside, running easily in the San

Pasqual Handicap, jockey Eric Guerin began to move just as Renown came over. Clipping heels, the colt fell hard, causing multiple fractures to the ulna or elbow, where the shoulder meets the foreleg. Tuffy was among the first to arrive on the scene, his toughness giving way to sorrow, as he recognized the critical need for a miracle.

Tuffy rode back to the barn in the horse ambulance, desperately trying to calm his friend. As required by the terms of the mortality policy, the insurer's veterinarian had to concur with any decision to euthanize Your Host. He did not. Both the track veterinarian and trainer Harry Daniels' vet recommended the horse be put down.

Lloyd's of London paid the policy, but in a rare twist of fate, took ownership and possession of the horse. Then began to save his life. Recovery was difficult and painful, but Your Host's will to live encouraged the attending veterinarians to employ extraordinary care. A continuous IV drip provided nutrition, electrolytes, and pain medication, 24 hours a day. Two vets were present at all times, monitoring their patient around the clock. It would be two more years before this brave descendant of The Tetrarch, through damsire Mahmoud, could take up stud duties.

Perhaps the greatest American thoroughbred of the twentieth century, five time Horse of the Year, Kelso, was sired by none other than Your Host. Tuffy got his miracle

The day after Christmas marked the beginning of the 41st Santa Anita meeting (1981-1982).

Never one to obligate himself to a jock, most of whom could ride, but only a few had what it takes to gallop; Whittingham was quick to match Crash with Perrault, an English bred, that pulled like a freight train.

Charlie drew from a cadre of top jocks. Among them were Johnny Sellers, Manny Ycaza, Howard Grant, Alex Solis along with notables, Ralph Neves and Eddie Arcaro. Always willing to reach out to the seldom used, but nonetheless skillful jockey, Charlie teamed with Merlin Volzke and Larry Gilligan to win handicaps. But, whenever listed together in the program, the Whittingham-Shoemaker pairing was formidable, seldom to be denied.

Perrault began his career in France, where he won major handicaps at Longchamp, Saint Cloud, and Deauville, the premier tracks, before continuing his winning ways in California. Whittingham was convinced he could win the $200,000 Big Cap, if only he could contain the robust chestnut's energy in the mornings. In Crash, he found a solution, promising him a $1000 bonus, if Perrault won Santa Anita's signature race.

For that contest, Charlie would seek the services of one of the strongest jocks on the grounds, smart with a clock in his head, a good judge of pace, essential for the mile-and-one-quarter distance, but above all, a dedicated well-disciplined athlete.

A perennial leading trainer of stakes quality

horses, Charlie Whittingham sought a soft spot, where his star could benefit from a tightener, and let off some steam. It became obvious that Perrault was expending himself too much in the morning, despite his exercise rider's best efforts. The British import was entered in the Arcadia Handicap.

Coming off a win in the Arcadia, he came back to win the Santa Anita Handicap, with Laffit Pincay in the irons. Despite Perrault being disqualified and placed second for interference, Charlie generously handed Crash the promised bonus.

At this same time, Whittingham was prepping the Irish bred stakes winner, Erins Isle, with an eye toward the Eclipse award. Winner of the Ballymoss Group II stakes at The Curragh, he was to be campaigned exclusively in the U.S. for the rest of his career. A bearcat on the grass, galloping home the easiest of winners against America's toughest turfers, he claimed victories in the Sunset, San Luis Rey, San Juan Capistrano, and Grade I Hollywood Turf Invitational.

He was a finalist for turf champion, edged out by the immortal John Henry for the Eclipse. The year before, he lost out to stablemate Perrault. A deal was in the works for Erins Isle to return to Ireland to stand stud, at Ballymany. An agreement was not yet inked, when the stud manager called Whittingham on his barn phone. The Aga Khan's prized stallion, Shergar, had been stolen.

∽ ∽ ∽

CHAPTER TWENTY-ONE

THE UNTHINKABLE

"**E**mmet, come in here," commanded Cresswell, the tallest of the group. Pulling off his ski mask revealed a pockmarked face, broken nose, and a half-closed, unblinking eyelid, making him a suitable candidate for the cover of *Ring* magazine.

"Does me mamó and granda know you're here?" Emmet asked in response.

"Doubt it, we didn't make much noise when we drove in. Your place was the only one we could think of that had stalls," a sinister sneer punctuating the reply.

Only hours before, they had pulled groom Jim Fitzgerald from his cottage on the grounds of the Aga Khan's Ballymany Stud. Forced at gunpoint to lead the men to Shergar, then load him onto the trailer, he was pistol whipped and thrown into the back of their Ford Granada. One of the men watched for police, while following in Cresswell's Hillman. Semiconscious, Fitzgerald was dumped by the roadside, a short walk from the farm.

"What's going on?" questioned the apprehensive teenager.

"We bought this horse to take down to Tipperary, where we can sell him for a profit, to donate to our cause," Cresswell replied, implying membership in one of the groups opposed to a Northern Ireland ruled by Britain.

"In the middle of the night?"

"Look here," Cresswell said, impatiently, "we think his leg is broken. Might have to put him down."

"I'll just go up to the house and ring the vet," offered Emmet.

"No, you don't," Cresswell growled, grabbing the boy's arm. "We haven't the money for no vet."

"My granda's got an account with Dr. O' Maille. Besides, I've been working on the gallops at The Curragh, and I can pay him."

"Well, we wouldn't think of it. Tell you what, tho', hows about goin' up there an' fixin' us some sandwiches, an' bring back some beer," Cresswell demanded, rather than asked.

The interrupted hum of the refrigerator alerted the grandparent's to Emmet's presence. Immediately, he sought to calm them, denying there was any problem, only friends laying over with a horse.

Returning to the barn with a tray of sandwiches and a cooler of ale, Emmet was met by the devil incarnate. He watched as Cresswell washed some white pills down with a Smithwick. Great, Emmet thought, the man is a closet speed freak. Agitated by the benzedrine and scattered in his thinking, the frustration of the present concerns compounded his volatile behavior.

"Gimme one of them sandwiches," Cresswell ordered, holding on to a saddle rack to steady a spurt of dizziness.

"Are you alright?" asked the boy, worried about what to expect next.

"Yeah, I'm fine," Cresswell answered, taking a bite of homemade brown bread. "Good God, Kid! What did you put in here?" he shouted, spitting out the sandwich.

"Marmite!"

"For Chrissakes, Brits have been trying to poison this country with that stuff since the Easter Rising. I hate you, and that fuckin' horse," he stammered, taking another swig of Smithwicks.

Some of the men sought to re-assure the boy, saying they had seen Cresswell like this before and that he would not do him harm. As to the horse, they could not be so sure.

The men did not fool the boy. As he sat down beside Shergar's stall, he thought they were all scared of their unpredictable leader. Hardly able to quieten his own anxiety, Emmet tried talking to Shergar in calm, even tones.

The horse started to weave and run his stall with each outburst from his captor. Sweat appeared on Shergar's neck and ears, darkening his leather halter. White lather formed inside his elbows and between his hind legs. Increasingly stressed, he was at risk. Emmet worried, that if Cresswell didn't kill him, colic would.

In an explosive tirade, Cresswell ordered his

men to help start the Hillman. "I have a call to make an' need to drive back to the Maxol station to phone that ol' groom we had to rough up. I gave him a code, so I know whoever I negotiate with has the authority from the Aga Khan to make a deal."

"That's smart, boss," said one of the men.

"Shut up," Cresswell shouted, misinterpreting the remark as condescending. "I told you to always park this piece-of-shit facing downhill, not against a fuckin' hillside like now. You men push it, I'll jump in and pop the clutch. Fuckin' clowns," he swore, deriding his crew.

"But boss, it's 4:00 a.m. No one's going to be awake."

"Good," responded Cresswell, "the line won't be busy."

A flickering flood light reflecting off the foggy morning, gave a hint of eeriness to the blue and gold Maxol signage. Shergar's groom, Jim Fitzsimmons, was awakened by the ringing. He said he would telephone the stud manager, and someone would call back within the hour.

Parking the Hillman on a slight incline near the telephone booth, Cresswell awaited the call. AIB bank blinked 9-2-83 40°. Promptly at 5:00 a.m. the phone rang. A man with a slight Italian accent began reciting the code, then launched in with the Aga Khan's position, not giving Cresswell a chance to speak his terms.

"I am Fausto, your connection to His Highness the Aga Khan. I will communicate everything you tell me. Likewise, my words to you come directly from His Highness. I will be brief. There is no interest in ransoming Shergar. Every stud farm in Ireland will become some sort of cash cow. No stallion will be safe. The Irish breeding program, built up for a century, will be destroyed.

"There is another complicating issue. You may not be aware that right after being named European Horse of the Year, Shergar was syndicated for ten million pounds. Norwich Union and Lloyd's of London provided the mortality insurance. So, if you kill him, no one loses except you, and a couple of insurance companies."

"Can I say something?" interrupted an anxious Cresswell.

"Go ahead," came Fausto's terse response, his tone implying the futility of the request.

"We're asking for two million. It makes sense for the insurance companies to pay out that sum, instead of ten million. And what about all those words of praise by His Highness, calling Shergar the best in the world. I know he's got a ton of money, doesn't he have a heart?"

"Not in this instance," said Fausto, convincingly. "You can fall on your sword as far as His Highness is concerned."

"Is that it then?"

"That's it, unless you have anything more?" questioned Fausto.

"Yeah," answered Cresswell, "Fuck you!"

Steamed with vexation, Cresswell raged from within, barely able to restart the Hillman.

Pointing at Shergar when he arrived at the barn, he yelled, "kill that son-of-a-bitch." It was times like this that Cresswell was at his most dangerous.

"We're pullin' the plug. We can't count on the kid's granda staying silent much longer. This fuckin' fiasco is all on some *guido's* conscience!" he exclaimed, in a misguided rant. "WLR will break the news, anytime now."

"They're a pirate station, not given to keeping things quiet, while the police work their investigation," added one of the men.

Directing a crazed stare at Emmet, Cresswell shouted, "here, get on with it," handing a Steyr-Daimler Puch sub-machine gun toward the frightened youth.

"I can't," said the kid, refusing to take the weapon.

"Fine, I'll just go up to the house and you will wish you did."

"Please, God, help me," Emmet prayed, aloud.

"No, you've been saying you wanted to join The Brotherhood. Now's your chance. Here, take this, goddammit, and put him out of his misery," Cresswell screamed, forcing the semi-automatic into Emmet's hand.

"Are you fuckin' kidding me? I won't do that," Emmet protested, "I can't."

"Yes, you will, or I'll cut your throat. You know horses and he'll trust you. It'll go quick and easy, one shot should do it."

Scared for his life, Emmet, barely eighteen,

opened the stall door. The others stood back, as Cresswell passed around a pack of Carroll's.

"Please don't smoke in the barn," admonished Emmet.

The men laughed at the innocent in their midst. The rosy cheeked youngster could not foresee the depravity that lay ahead.

"This horse looks okay to me," he remarked, running his hand down the bay's foreleg. "Just some abrasions. Doesn't need a vet. I can take care of him."

"Fuck it, Kid, I've just about had enough of you," screamed the ringleader. "Get in there and kill the bastard."

"I know this horse. That big white blaze. I saw him paraded up main street in Newbridge, when the Aga Khan retired him to stud. This is Shergar."

"You don't say," Cresswell said with a menacing smirk, pulling a dagger from its sheath.

Faced with an unthinkable choice, the frightened youth aimed the weapon. Never a good marksman, the close range made no difference. His hands shaking, the first few shots tore open the flesh, enraging the animal.

"Finish him," yelled a vicious chorus.

Crying uncontrollably, Emmet begged Cresswell to let him stop.

"Too late, quit your sniffling," came the angry response. "If this isn't done soon, I won't be responsible for what happens next," Cresswell bullied.

The threat had an emetic effect. Amid the tears and vomit, the youth fired again and again, until the horse collapsed. Attempting to get up in a desperate effort at survival, Shergar crashed through a side wall.

A light went on in the main house and Emmet was ordered to go up to re-assure his grandparents.

"Don't be long," instructed Cresswell, "we have more work to do." Turning to the others, he motioned them to extricate the horse from the broken boards.

"Now what?" they asked, unable to anticipate their leader's next command.

"Chop him up, you twits. There's an ax and saw above the tool table. Hurry," demanded Cresswell.

Blood spattered clothes and reddened eyes, belied any efforts by Emmet to assuage his grandparent's fears. But, these were troubled times, and Emmet implored them not to call the police. Returning to the stables, he saw the dismembered Shergar. Emmet heaved uncontrollably.

"Come on. Don't be such a sissy. What you did is the same as slaughtering a horse for a French dinner table. Where's your car?" Cresswell demanded.

"The Vauxall over there," answered Emmet, afraid his involvement was not yet over.

"Get it," commanded Cresswell. Looking at the others, he directed Shergar's legs be placed in the boot; the neck and body on the back seat.

Emmet believed these men were responsible for an unaccountable number of wounded and killed, including women and children. Hardened to the spectre of bloodshed and the murder of innocents, in the name of freedom, there was still a sense of revulsion among them, having partaken in the killing of a national hero.

Emmet got behind the wheel of the Vauxhall, with Cresswell pointing a Falklands War souvenir handgun at his mid-section. Grabbing a spade, hoe, and rake, the others followed in the grandfather's Iveco Daily. Cresswell directed the boy to drive to a desolate area, uninhabitable because of the boggy ground. The tides and ever present rain caused it to shift like quicksand.

"Start shoveling," Cresswell barked at the men.

Pointing the Argentine made Browning Hi-Power at Emmet's head, as he stood near the rim of the pit, the malevolent leader smiled, then said, "In you go."

"Why me?" questioned the lad.

"You ask too many questions. Know too much for your own good," replied Cresswell in a chilling matter-of-fact tone.

"Besides, you killed Shergar!" Cresswell exclaimed, determined to end the conversation.

"*Téigh, trasna ort féin*, Cresswell, or whatever your name is," Emmet cursed, repeating, "Go fuck yourself!" before tumbling backward, the deafening report from the 9 mm semi-automatic, shattering the stillness of the pre-dawn air.

Looking at one of the men, Cresswell ordered

him to fetch enough hydrofluoric acid, "to clean this mess up. Don't get it on you. That stuff will eat you like a piranha." The gangbanger didn't have to be warned twice. He had seen the spilled acid delacerate a man's torso, killing him within minutes.

"The cops will find Jimmy Hoffa, before they find those two," added a cocksure Cresswell.

To another, he ordered, "take the Vauxhall up to Belfast. Torch it. The RUC won't investigate. It will just be one of many burned out cars on the street. Take the train back. I'll go to the stable, pick up the Granada and dump the horse box. Then I'm going to breakfast," said their sociopathic leader, exuding a sense of accomplishment, despite failing to obtain a ransom. The man was deluded by his own dark side.

The 8:00 a.m. news broadcast alarmed the grandfather, who already feared for Emmet's safety. Reports of Shergar's disappearance were now being aired on television, uniting the nation in shock and disbelief. Bolting from the kitchen table, energized by the urgency at hand, he grabbed his old .32 Mauser pistol, telling his wife to stay behind, as he rushed down to the barn.

Instantly, he was aware there had been a violent struggle. Cigarette butts and beer bottles littered the entryway. Drag marks to the outside were deep and bloodied. The open stall door revealed a crushed water bucket, blood red straw, and broken sideboards. An aluminum shoe, still nailed to hoof wall, wedged itself in the seam of the metal feed tub. Emmet was nowhere in sight, not responding to calls.

By the time the old man got up to the house, he could hardly breathe, panic combined with exhaustion. He asked his wife to telephone the police, knowing that it could mean certain death for his grandson, if any of the gang stayed behind to watch the house. What else could he do? he asked himself. For so many in these times, fate often called for unexpected death. Being in the wrong place could be a mortal mistake.

Within days after the kidnapping, the rumor mill was operating at full capacity. The police continuously chased phantom sightings, looking into numerous stables and cow barns, unearthing any fresh plot of ground.

After the first two weeks, the lead detective admitted they had no new clues other than the ones discovered on that first day; the bloodied stall, the aluminum shoe, the broken sidewall, and numerous shell casings. He purposefully withheld information as to the discovery of an automatic gun clip to preserve the integrity of the investigation.

Anyone confessing to the crime would have to identify the weapon. More than a few wackos would claim to be the culprit. But more importantly, there was concern that disclosing the clip came from a Steyr-Daimler would result in warfare among the horse loving Irish and a faction of the IRA. The gun was the assault rifle of choice used by the Provisional IRA. There was already a suspicion the IRA was involved; the ammunition clip would have been strong circumstantial proof.

It is not easy to transport and hide a horse, especially one marked distinctively like Shergar. Most people surmised he was dead and buried. The insurance companies, however, required ironclad verification, rather than rely on supposition, refusing to pay out to the syndicate members. They have remained steadfast in this refusal.

CHAPTER TWENTY-TWO

THE WONDER

The following Santa Anita meeting (1982-1983), Team Whittingham tried again to win the Big Cap; this time with The Wonder, a multiple Goup I winner imported from France just prior to the 1983 New Year. Typical of the European horses normally trained on long gallop paths, The Wonder balked, unable to relax on the busy Santa Anita racetrack, sometimes crowded with over fifty horses training at any given time.

Crash reported for work every morning at 5:45 a.m. in order to get The Wonder exercised before dawn. As he looked over the board to see what other horses he was to gallop, Charlie called out.

"Hey, weren't you around Shergar?"

"Yes sir, I saw all his big wins over there," Crash answered proudly. "He took your breath away."

"Shergar was kidnapped yesterday, at least that's when the criminals phoned the Aga Khan with a ransom demand. There's a lot of confusion about the facts, and nothing about it on the news here, yet."

Visibly shaken with worry over the kind, gentle Champion he had come to know, Crash asked if he could busy himself cleaning tack instead of taking horses to the track.

"No sense in you getting hurt doing a job, where you need your wits about you at all times," Charlie said sympathetically, consenting to the request.

More details emerged on radio and television throughout the day. Quickly, Shergar's fate was becoming the topic of conversation on the backstretch. The story was spreading through barns across the globe, reaching the Canadian provinces, down to Mexico City's Hipodromo de las Americas, moving south to Panama, Brazil, Peru, Chile, and Argentina, horse racing strongholds. Europe, the UK, Australia, Asia, and Japan got word the day before. Time zones determined who first heard new developments, from that point on it was telephones. Newspapers were a day behind. But, no one heard the news quicker than someone living in County Kildare.

Media accuracy was suspect, either understated or sensationalized. Some reports were mixed. 'Shergar was alive, awaiting release upon payment of ransom.' Others were less optimistic, claiming, 'the Aga Khan has refused to pay anything.' 'Negotiations have broken off.' All accounts blamed the IRA, apparently indistinguishable from the Official IRA, Provisional IRA, or an ordinary band of criminals.

Grace returned home after an emotionally draining day. Already fragile, she broke into tears upon hearing of Shergar's abduction, disbelieving anyone could do him harm.

"Sounds like some rogue Provo or IRA caper led by a loose cannon," stated Crash. "Both organizations are military in nature, with a strict code of honor and discipline. Criminal actions like that aren't done in a vacuum. They're meticulously planned and well executed, approved by the top command, with a solid exit strategy.

"Operative squads or cells don't unilaterally decide to take on actions against Irish citizens or Irish economic institutions. Jim Fitzgerald and Ballymany Stud were just that.

"Think about it for a minute. The Irish hold their horses sacred, like the people of India honor their cows. Neither organization would give a green light to stealing or killing any horse, much less an iconic Irish bred Champion like Shergar. They have to know the fallout will set their agenda back to 1916, if there is a connection, drying up Irish American financing and alienating their political supporters. What, they get two million, and in doing so spurn fifty million, plus boatloads of arms? Not likely.

"Compare this with the assassination of Mountbatten four years ago. No less than a member of royalty, the Queen's first cousin, Admiral of the Fleet, and Commander of the British troops, gets blown to bits along with women and children. Talk about exit strategy, the bomb maker was seventy miles away, when it was detonated.

"However, immediately afterward, the Provos claimed responsibility. Historically, the IRA and Provos have not been shy about stepping up to the plate, no matter the number of casualties or how heinous the crime. And, they don't wait a week to assess the fallout. They announce their culpability before the smoke clears.

"Remember reading the BBC report, after Mountbatten was killed? They attributed a statement to the IRA, saying, 'this is one of the discriminate ways we can bring attention to the English people, the continued occupation of our country.' That is the reason they always claim responsibility."

"There is really no such crime as kidnapping a horse. It is theft of personal property, the ransom demand is extortion. Grabbing Fitzgerald out of his house is assault and kidnapping, but no worse than what happens every day here in LA," said Grace, with lawyerlike certainty.

"Believe me," Crash began, "if the IRA had anything to do with this, they would not need to ask someone to show them where Shergar was stabled. Nor would they need Fitzgerald to load the horse. They have plenty of sympathizers, who are good horsemen.

"Hell, they could of sent along a veterinarian team. And, they do not assign anyone to a job that can't handle it. Also, they would have known before hand, the Aga Khan no longer had full control; that the syndicate members and insurance carriers would have to be involved.

"Causing injury to animals is cruelty, often-times not even a felony. The penalty is the same whether it is a horse or a cat. Killing someone else's animal is destruction of private property, same as smashing their car window. Depending on the replacement value, it may only be a misdemeanor. Of course, the prosecutor might add a charge of malicious mischief," added Grace.

"Yeah, agreed Crash, the Provos or IRA aren't laying low because they fear criminal prosecution. What would they get? 5 or 10 years max. That's nothing to those guys; they can do that standing on their heads, with or without blankets."

"So what do think?" questioned Grace. "Why don't they deny any involvement?"

"They don't do denials. Negatives are hard to prove. They do admissions. Otherwise they would be spending all their energy denying involvement in all the street crimes committed in Ireland. Their targets are political, designated to advance the cause of a Free Ireland.

"They may bomb buildings, which house polit-ical oppressors or organizations like the UDR or Royal Ulster Constabulary that specialize in preying on innocents, beating or murdering.

"They may execute or assassinate actual perpe-trators of hostilities or depredations against the Irish people. Or the target may be a symbolic representative of oppression, like Mountbatten."

"Well if not the IRA, then who did it?" Grace pressed on.

"Maybe common criminals, trying to cash in on Shergar. Two years ago, a couple of get-rich-quick guys in Kentucky, pulled Fanfreluche out of her pasture at Claiborne farm, a preeminent facility. She was Canada's Horse-of-the-Year and America's Champion Three-Year-Old Filly. Bred to Secretariat, she had been pronounced in foal.

"Once the FBI got involved, the thieves panicked, and took her to a riding stable in Tennessee. They paid the board with a personal check. Were they slick, or what? When the stable manager heard of the theft, she turned Fanfreluche and the cancelled check over to the local Sheriff.

"Then there was the case of Carnauba in 1975, Italy's Champion Three-Year-Old Filly. She was found at a meat packing yard near Milan, destined for slaughter, after her abductors abandoned their scheme. They too had sought a ransom from a multi-billionaire owner, Nelson Bunker Hunt, who refused.

"My best guess, based on the simple fact that history repeats itself, is neither the IRA nor Provos had anything to do with it. There was no viable exit strategy, and any juvenile delinquent could have devised a better plan than the botched job at Ballymany. If several maverick members took it upon themselves, then it wasn't sanctioned.

"And, if a rogue group within the IRA did it, the Brotherhood will find out long before the *Garda*. The perpetrators will be court martialed.

They would have been an embarrassment to the highly disciplined order of the IRA. Their conviction would never be reported."

"Then what would happen to them?" asked Grace, a staunch opponent of the death penalty.

"The IRA doesn't have any prisons. They surely don't lease space at Castlereagh," answered Crash, not wishing to elaborate, avoiding one more crying jag.

"Remember the Miami Showband? The Ulster Volunteer Force tried to frame the IRA for transportation of explosives. They wouldn't think twice about framing the IRA for Shergar; no doubt they could use the money, and like with the Showband killings, they would have protection, unless of course IRA spies infiltrating the RUC or UVF found them out."

"Does the IRA have spies?" Grace asked, in a hushed tone.

"Yes, just like the CIA or FBI infiltrates the Hell's Angels, NAACP, Students for a Democratic Society, Black Panthers or any other group the ghost of J. Edgar Hoover deems to be a threat to national security."

"Why defend the IRA? I thought you were English."

"I am, by birth. But, if you happened to be born in Beijing, would that make you Chinese?" Crash did not seek an answer, having made his point.

"To use a Pádraig Pearse phrase, the IRA has made many 'blood sacrifices' to get most of the country under Home Rule. In many respects, daily life is better than it was before the War of Independence. Far from perfect, now with The Troubles, I'll grant you.

"As to defending the IRA, they have committed their share of atrocities, putting men, women and children in their graves. Unfortunately, throughout history, freedom has never been gained without bloodshed, that of the rulers, kings or czars, and the ruled: women and children, boys and men. But, that is war, and as George once told me, 'war is depraved.' As to Shergar, I just don't want to see the IRA get a bum rap."

EPILOGUE

Crash and Grace continued their lives in Los Angeles, with Crash galloping horses for Charlie Whittingham. The Wonder encountered traffic trouble in the Big Cap. Following his last place finish, he reeled off three straight Grade I & II stakes victories. Grace dedicated herself to social services for children in need of protection, transferring to the familiar denizens of Watts, where she could be the most effective. The couple eventually began a family of their own.

Did billboards such as the one in the Sundown Town of Hawthorne, California really exist? Shamefully, yes.

Thomas McMahon was released after serving 18 years of a 32 year prison sentence, under the terms of the Good Friday Agreement signed in 1998. The Agreement also called for the decommissioning of weapons arming paramilitary groups, including the IRA. It also recognized Northern Ireland's referendum to remain within the United Kingdom. Further, the terms called for the parties to use exclusively democratic and peaceful means of resolving differences on political issues.

It was to be another seven years before a complete decommissioning of weapons would take place, bringing a strained peace. The Six Counties are now governed by the Northern Ireland Executive, its powers granted by the United Kingdom. Whole neighborhoods remain segregated by religion. Fences continue to delineate the boundaries for Catholics and Protestants, who attend separate schools.

George Brent can still be seen on television stations that offer movies from Hollywood's bygone years. He was the owner, trainer, and breeder of Shimmering Star, a daughter of Waterline, second in the Goose Girl Stakes and winner of the Las Flores Handicap. Debonair and charming, George is often shown on screen sporting the pencil thin moustache, popularized by Clark Gable and himself.

Was he really an IRA operative under Michael Collins? Absolutely.

Typically, informers were targeted for removal during The Troubles. No doubt some people were selected merely for the company they kept, their religious views, or their politics. So many went missing, history has assigned them a name, *The Disappeared.* Today, The Independent Commission for the Location of Victim's Remains coordinates searches and keeps a confidential data base.

No one involved in Shergar's abduction has

ever been identified, nor have his remains been discovered. Peat bogs near saltwater can be as much as twelve feet deep. The salt and minerals in the sea spray infuse the soil with humic acid. Waterlogged and acidic, the bogs shut out oxygen and bacteria, halting decomposition. Layers of sphagnum moss cover the low lying land, serving to help keep intact anything below. Unwittingly, Cresswell chose to preserve proof of his diabolical crime rather than bury the evidence.

The description of events and Shergar's demise is a fictional portrayal, based in part on accounts gleaned from the investigative reporting of others. The bogs were favored by the IRA, Provos, UDR, UDF and any number of criminals seeking to dispose of their victims, hidden forever, save perhaps from future archaeologists.

There is no question that Shergar would have become a prominent sire, with a high demand for his offspring. His first and only foal crop included six stakes winners. His best was Authaal, born in Kentucky, then returned to Ireland, where he sold as a yearling for three million guineas, two years before winning the Irish St. Leger. Through Authaal, Shergar continues to be an influence in a limited number of broodmares.

ABOUT The AUTHOR

His family immigrated from County Meath to escape the hardships of Ireland. Stephen Halstead was born in the UK. A lifelong racetracker, he has raced quarterhorses, and thoroughbreds across Canada, in Mexico and throughout the United States. He previously authored *Everywhere Spirit*. He is currently working on his next book, *The Diver, Native that is.*

CPSIA information can be obtained
at www.ICGtesting.com
Printed in the USA
FSOW01n0526301215
15023FS

9 781591 461739